Dureena was in an air duct, a square pipe that sloped upward at a steep angle. Setting her feet, she made her way through it, finding handholds, slithering snakelike, around one bend and then another, until at last she came to an egress that dropped her in a wholly unfamiliar area.

Cautiously, she poked her head out. She was still in Down Below—that much was clear—in a place filled with battered garbage cans and discarded boxes. There seemed to be no one around. She pulled herself out. Then she looked around again—and froze.

Someone was pressing a gun to the back of her head.

Whoever could get behind her that way was good— very good. She was about to congratulate him on his stealth. But the man spoke first.

"Good night," Rolf said. And he coldcocked her with the gun butt . . .

Published by Ballantine Books:

CREATING BABYLON 5 by David Bassom

Babylon 5 Season-by-Season Guides by Jane Killick
#1 SIGNS AND PORTENTS
#2 THE COMING OF SHADOWS
#3 POINT OF NO RETURN
#4 NO SURRENDER, NO RETREAT
#5 THE WHEEL OF FIRE*

BABYLON 5 SECURITY MANUAL

BABYLON 5: IN THE BEGINNING by Peter David
BABYLON 5: THIRDSPACE by Peter David
BABYLON 5: A CALL TO ARMS by Robert Sheckley

The Saga of Psi Corps by J. Gregory Keyes
BABYLON 5: DARK GENESIS
BABYLON 5: DEADLY RELATIONS*

*forthcoming

5 BABYLON™

A Call to Arms

By Robert Sheckley

Based on
the screenplay by
J. Michael Straczynski

™

A Del Rey® Book

THE BALLANTINE PUBLISHING GROUP • NEW YORK

A Del Rey® Book
Published by The Ballantine Publishing Group
TM & copyright © 1999 by Warner Bros.

www.randomhouse.com/delrey/

Library of Congress Catalog Card Number: 98-96783

ISBN 0-345-43155-3

Manufactured in the United States of America

First Edition: January 1999

10   9   8   7   6   5   4   3   2   1

A Call to Arms

—— chapter 1 ——

It was a neutral kind of a darkness to which John Sheridan opened his eyes. The first sense that kicked in was smell. The place was immediately characterized by a lack of smell.

But as soon as he concentrated, Sheridan picked up faint traces of a familiar and not offensive scent. Minbari. Of course. He was on a Minbari cruiser.

He opened his eyes in the small darkened room they had assigned him. He noticed the luminous dial of a clock on a facing wall. It was just two minutes before the time he had asked them to call him.

He still retained the military training that had been instilled in him over the years. No matter how much time passed, he would never forget the beefy captain of cadets back at the Academy, his voice full of mock irony as he drawled, "Gentlemen, shall we rise and shine? Or shall we linger in our beds awhile longer, thus inviting company punishment at the best, courts-martial at the worst?" And out they'd pile, all the new cadets, Sheridan among them, ready to face the new day and whatever it might bring.

Discipline had been so deeply ingrained in Sheridan

that nothing could erase it. Even when he was off duty, even while he and Delenn had been on their honeymoon, he had always been up before dawn—no matter what time dawn was on whatever planet he happened to be stationed. And not just up but awake, alert, bright-eyed and bushy-tailed, ready to face whatever the new day might bring.

His wrist link went off, pulling him back to the present. He toggled it.

"President Sheridan?" It was the voice of the duty officer. Sheridan remembered him from the mess table the previous night. A large, cheerful Minbari with a good sense of humor. He had told several lively jokes, not all of them comprehensible to an Earther.

But his voice was formal and serious now. "This is the call you requested. The *White Star* is within visual range."

"Yes, thank you," Sheridan said. "I'll be up to the bridge presently."

He rolled out of bed. The bathroom was a tiny cubicle; the Minbari wasted no time installing amenities on their capital ships, even for the senior officers. He took a cold shower, enjoying the needle spray of water stinging his skin. He dried off and wrapped himself in a towel, then shaved, leaving his trim salt-and-pepper beard intact, and tried to remember his dream of the night before.

It had been the same dream again, like the ones he'd experienced so many times recently. The ones he couldn't quite remember. The ones that felt so important but always vanished as soon as he woke up, leaving only lingering hints.

He dressed, and mused. This particular series of dreams had been going on for a while now, though he couldn't remember just how long. The one last night had been like the others: it inspired a feeling that someone was trying to warn him of something important, to break through the daytime barrier in his mind. There was the familiar sense—of something urgent that he needed to remember, something he had to do, and quickly, quickly, not a moment to be lost.

But what was it?

He hadn't told anyone about the dreams. Some people thought he was crazy enough as it was, with his hunches that were too complex and multileveled to explain. And besides, there was nothing to tell. Whenever he woke up, his dreams dissolved before he could grasp them. But even though he wasn't sure of their content, he knew they were important, and he couldn't escape the feeling that something or someone was trying to communicate with him.

Although he considered himself a rational man, Sheridan didn't discount the importance of dreams. So often they were portents of things to come. More than once, dreams had played a crucial part in his life. But he didn't like to overstress their importance. He knew that some dreams, while they might seem important, simply weren't visionary.

He had even studied the subject in what he laughingly referred to as his spare time, looking up the subject in the big on-line library maintained on the Babylon 5 space station, where he had begun his presidency, only five years earlier.

Some of the ancients had documented interesting

ideas on dreams. Iamblichus, for example, was a Greek
who had devoted his studies to the Egyptian mysteries
of Serapis. He had written a book on dream explanation
and interpretation as early as A.D. 235. The next prominent figure had been Marsilio Ficino, writing in Italy
during the Renaissance. Still later, the Frenchman Binet
had been an early pioneer in dream research. His work
had been extended by the French Desoille, Sigmund
Freud, and C. G. Jung.

Freud had been responsible for the line of reasoning
that claimed dreams were reenactments of childhood
scenes. The Jungians seemed to feel dreams related to
figures in what they called the "archetypal consciousness." Writers like Hillman and Cobb felt dreams were
a road into an inner landscape of the underworld, which
they felt every person possessed. One school held that
dreams were composed of odds and ends thrown up by
the mind, things thought or seen during the day that
hadn't quite reached the threshold of consciousness.

But some authorities, like Jannig and Vierese, believed there were visionary dreams, too, scenes and visions viewed by the mind as it traveled in many
dimensions in its nightly wanderings. Their theories
had gained new popularity in 2115, with the confirma-
tion of telepathy.

Sheridan suspected his recent dreams didn't fit any
of the standard categories. It was almost as if someone
or something was trying to *send* him a dream, or make
contact with him while he was sleeping. He wondered,
uneasily, if his dream experiences might in fact have
something to do with telepathy. He sincerely hoped
not. His experiences with the Psi Corps had left him

with a deep suspicion of this wild talent, and like so many, he maintained a fear of falling under its spell.

It was true that the Psi Corps had been reformed and transformed. There was more freedom for telepaths, and mingling between telepaths and normals was no longer forbidden. Telepaths no longer had to wear gloves and special uniforms, but still, each telepath was scanned every six months to make sure they hadn't been infringing on the rights of normals. And Sheridan still held many of his old suspicions.

Whatever the explanation, dreams haunted his sleep most nights and left him wondering about them during the day.

He hadn't been sleeping well recently. He attributed that in part to the fact that he was so far from Delenn. His wife was on Minbar, her home planet, and he was on a Minbari cruiser, en route to a rendezvous with Michael Garibaldi.

He and Delenn had become very close, almost psychically attuned to one another. Sometimes he felt incomplete without her by his side. But she was acting as a combined vice president and first lady for the Interstellar Alliance of Races.

The vague dreams made him uneasy, and though he didn't care to acknowledge the feeling, he wished he could talk it over with Delenn. But neither could spare the time—the very nature of their responsibilities frequently kept them apart. She couldn't leave Minbar on a whim; her presence was necessary there. And their unique relationship allowed them to carry on in two places at once. Though Sheridan sometimes wished otherwise, he knew they were both considered indispensable.

But he also had learned, from his military background, his lifetime of service, not to take himself *too* seriously, no matter what his rank or position. Men and women came and went, but the workings of the universe went on—the all-important mechanics of civilization, great tasks such as creating peace and order where war and chaos had been before. If he wasn't around to perform those tasks, then someone else would be.

That's what he believed, but it wasn't the sort of thing you talked about.

So he straightened his clothing and prepared to go to the bridge.

Indispensable? Maybe not in a general sense. But in a limited way, yes, since events hinged on the lives of individuals. He and Delenn were pivotal people. They were the first leaders of the Interstellar Alliance—people who, due to their placement, not necessarily to their abilities, were crucial to the unfolding of events.

Delenn was currently organizing and orchestrating the events of the grand celebration that would mark the fifth anniversary of the Alliance. And he? He was having dreams that he couldn't remember. Not any of their content, not even their mood. There was only one thing his dreams seemed to be telling him—that something big was going to happen, and it wouldn't be a party.

Finishing his preparations, and skipping breakfast, Sheridan came directly to the bridge of the cruiser. The

White Star to which he was transferring was already within visual range. The sleek, hawklike form of these ships never ceased to thrill him.

The bridge was a scene of quiet, organized activity as the Minbari navigator made the final adjustments to match his ship's speed to that of the *White Star*. All around him there was the hushed discipline of a well-run ship, officers and crew attending to their duties with a minimum of conversation.

The Minbari commander was aware of Sheridan as soon as he stepped onto the bridge. The commander had arrived early to be sure of greeting him properly. He'd had a talk with his officers late last night, after Sheridan had turned in, just to be sure they'd know how to act. He'd told them, "President Sheridan likes to keep things casual. I don't suppose he knows it, but that presents more of a problem than if he were a stickler for strict discipline. If he addresses any of you, respond in a friendly manner, but always with reserve and respect. Do I make myself clear?"

Sure, sir, we'll deal with him just like we deal with you, his junior officers were thinking, but by no means saying. The Minbari commander, though well liked, simply didn't realize that he was a problem for his junior officers just like Sheridan was a problem for him.

But Sheridan wasn't in a very conversational mood that morning. He nodded pleasantly enough to the commander and his bridge crew.

"Everything in order for the transfer?"

"Yes, sir!" the Minbari commander responded. "The *White Star* is in place, and our launch is ready to take you over to her."

"Might as well get on with it, then," Sheridan said, and started toward the lock, the Minbari commander accompanying him.

"Good luck, sir," the Minbari said when they reached the lock entrance. "It's been a pleasure escorting you here. Hope to see you again soon."

"I look forward to it," Sheridan said. He gave the commander a friendly nod and entered the lock.

Now that there was work to do, he put aside his musings. All that was left of his dream was a vague premonition. But not even that gave him a clue as to just what was to come.

—— chapter 2 ——

Sheridan wasn't the only one having trouble with his dreams. Michael Garibaldi was also having a dream, in his darkened cubicle aboard the *White Star*, just before Sheridan's arrival. Unlike Sheridan, Garibaldi was not one to analyze his dreams, and he never considered researching them.

And where Sheridan's dream had been vague and uncertain, Garibaldi's was clear and definite.

In his dream, Garibaldi was in a bar back on Earth. He was in a run-down part of a large city—New York, maybe, near the approaches to the Lincoln Tunnel. It was nighttime, and there was a glow in the air from the streetlights that lit the long avenue.

He'd been going somewhere in his car, driving along, calm, happy, pleased with life in general. But he'd stopped because he suddenly remembered he needed to make a phone call. A call to whom, about what? The dream hadn't specified.

He was in an inconvenient place to stop: a neighborhood that had never seen better days. It was a dark place, filled with run-down buildings. Garbage was strewn on the streets.

9

Garibaldi didn't even question why he didn't have a car phone. He simply didn't, so he stopped near a dimly lit bar. He wasn't going in there for a drink. That was the farthest thing from his mind. He was off the booze, hadn't had a drop in years. No, he simply had to make this telephone call.

The street was dark, but the bar was even darker when he went in. Overhead spotlights above the curved bar sent out pools of light in an otherwise dark room. And it was quiet, with that introspective silence that places devoted to serious drinking seem to generate.

There were half a dozen patrons at the bar, four men, two women. They all seemed frozen in place, like marionettes. The bartender, in white jacket and black tie, was standing motionless behind the bar, like he was sleepwalking or something.

"What can I get you?" the bartender asked.

"Hey, I just want to use the phone," Garibaldi said. "You got one here?"

The bartender didn't answer. Garibaldi was about to repeat his request, this time in a louder voice, when it occurred to him to look around. There were two more people in the place than he'd noticed originally, both of them standing.

One guy was lounging by the pinball machine in a corner of the bar near the phone booth. He was tall and skinny and wore glasses. He had on a sports jacket but wasn't wearing a necktie. He was grinning. He had a sawed-off shotgun tucked under his arm.

It took Garibaldi a moment to register the gun, so casually was the man holding it, and a moment more to realize that something was very wrong.

Then he noticed the other man.

This man was standing to one side of the bar, in shadow. He stepped forward into the beam of one of the overhead spotlights. He was a big, hard-looking guy, stocky, broad-shouldered, with a scar down the left side of his face. He was holding a large blued-steel automatic in one hand, dangling it negligently at his side. He had a hat pulled down flat over his large head. He had on a glen-plaid suit, cut sharply. An expensive-looking camel hair topcoat was draped over his shoulders.

"Looks like I came by at the wrong time," Garibaldi said, trying to seem casual. "I'll just make my call somewhere else, and have a nice day . . ."

"Naw, stick around," the scar-faced man said. There was no special tone of menace in his voice, but Garibaldi stopped.

"What?" Garibaldi asked.

"Just don't make trouble," the scar-faced man said. "We're not here to hurt anyone . . . else." He lifted his chin toward the bar. "We already done what we came to do."

That was when Garibaldi made out the crumpled shape on the floor.

He nodded. It looked like a mob hit. He had missed the killing action. But it looked like the trouble was over. Garibaldi relaxed slightly. And then it came.

The broad-shouldered man said, "Me and my buddy will be leaving now. Just sit tight and you'll be all right.

We'll just walk out, and you'll stay where you are and nobody gets hurt. Okay?"

Garibaldi nodded vigorously.

The scar-faced man went on, "Just to show you there's no hard feelings, I'm going to buy everyone a drink. Bartender, drinks for everyone. Make it Scotch. Your best Scotch."

Garibaldi's thoughts began to tumble quickly through his head: *This can't be happening to me. I'm off the booze, I'm doing fine, and this bozo is going to force me to drink again.*

Garibaldi was beginning to get annoyed. He wasn't going back to drinking! No matter what they thought, he wasn't going to take that drink. He'd just have to explain it to the scar-faced guy and take his chances.

The bartender poured his drink. When Garibaldi saw the whiskey, brimming to the top of the shot glass, with one amber drop trickling down the side, he thought it looked mighty enticing. Suddenly the memory of good times returned to him. He sure would love a Scotch! But no one was going to force him to drink it.

He saw that the others at the bar had downed their shots. They looked relieved, like they'd done what was necessary and were now safe.

His was the only full shot glass on the bar.

"You got any problem drinking with me?" the scar-faced man asked.

"Nope," Garibaldi said, deciding this wasn't the time to try to explain, not with a blued-steel automatic picking up winks of light as it waved in his face. He raised the shot glass and downed the contents, and a feeling of pleasure, of relief, flooded him. He was drinking because he had to, to save his life! No one could blame him for that . . .

And then he woke up.

—— chapter 3 ——

A half hour later, Garibaldi came to the bridge of the *White Star* feeling grumpy and out of sorts—a typical mood for him. He was dressed in dark, shapeless clothing. It went with his mood.

Once, in a circus back on Earth, many years ago when he had been a youngster, he had visited a sideshow. There had been an old gypsy woman, her head covered in a glittering kerchief, her eyes deep and hidden from the light.

"Can you read my palm?" Garibaldi had asked, with a wise-guy smirk, holding out his hand.

"I don't need to," the gypsy said. "I can see your fortune in your face."

"Yeah? And what does it tell you?"

"That you won't be happy as you go through life, especially with your truculent temperament, but you will have interesting adventures, and you'll get a lot of the best lines."

"Hey, that's good enough for me," Garibaldi had said, and he had gone off whistling, hands in his pockets.

Had that really happened? Or had he dreamed it?

He shrugged off the thought and went to the window. He saw a dot detach itself from the Minbari cruiser and start toward the *White Star*. It was the shuttle with Sheridan aboard, moving slowly toward them, its rear jets a stabbing red plume. Sheridan was right on time.

Garibaldi glanced around the *White Star*'s bridge. Everything seemed to be in order. There was a soft hum of purposeful activity. Human and Minbari Rangers were working at their consoles; data was flowing across the readout screens. Everybody seemed to know just what to do. Garibaldi wished he could say the same for himself. In his experience, life was one long improvisation broken up by unaccountable interludes.

"That's him," Garibaldi remarked to the Human Ranger standing by and awaiting his orders. "Move us away as soon as he's aboard. And tell 'em to have dinner ready. It's been a long trip, and he's bound to be hungry. And even if he's not, I am."

Fifteen minutes later, John Sheridan was aboard. Garibaldi greeted him with barely concealed warmth. Sheridan was one of his favorite people. It was not always easy for Garibaldi to put on his usual gruff face: his admiration for the man made that difficult. Still, he did his best.

He led Sheridan inside and brought him to a booth in the dining room. There was no delay. The kitchen staff had been waiting for this. The first course seemed to be miniature enchiladas in a simple white sauce. Garibaldi ate his with good appetite, but noticed that Sheridan was toying with his. Garibaldi liked Minbari food, but suspected it might not agree with the president, not even when it had been cleared through xeno-cuisine substitutes.

Now, putting down his fork, Sheridan said, "Michael, it's good to see you. How are things going on Mars?"

"Couldn't be better," Garibaldi said. "Never figured myself for the corporate type. I mean, me, running one of the ten biggest corporations on Mars? But I'm having a ball."

"Well," Sheridan said, "I appreciate you getting into this, Michael. I haven't been able to stay as involved with the construction on the new ships as I'd've liked."

"Hey, c'mon, you've got a galactic empire to run . . . Leave the nuts and bolts to the other guys. Kicking butt is what I do for a living."

"Then you've talked to the head of construction . . . what's his name . . . Drake?"

Garibaldi gave a sour smile. In his mind's eye he conjured up Drake's image: a small, efficient man who worked hard at being affable, yet with a certain prissiness about him, and a meanness based, perhaps, on a fear of things getting out of order, out of control. Not endearing qualities.

"Talked, yelled, screamed . . . He's a bright guy, but he's one of those people who wants everything perfect before he does anything. So nothing gets done."

"Roast leg of lamb," Sheridan commented as the waiter wheeled over a cart. "You know my tastes."

"And it's nice when they coincide with my own," Garibaldi replied.

"Well, I understand Drake's caution," Sheridan said. "Reverse-engineering Minbari and Vorlon technology so it'll work with Human tech . . . it's never been done before."

Garibaldi nodded, unconvinced. "Maybe so. Once we're done you're going to have the leanest, meanest fleet on the block. Of course, all the other races are gonna go nuts when they find out."

"I know," Sheridan said. "That's why we're doing this in secret. If they knew we were building a whole new class of destroyer, they'd be all over us. Fortunately, we've got a pretty good smoke screen to hide the funding, and Delenn's keeping everyone's attention back on Minbar getting ready for the anniversary. Nobody knows we're here."

Just then a Minbari Ranger came over. "Mr. President . . . we're clear of all the shipping lanes. We can jump at any time."

"Good," Sheridan said. "Proceed."

The Ranger saluted sharply, turned, and left. There was a subtle change that rippled through the people in the dining room. It was as though somehow, almost telepathically, everyone was aware that the *White Star* was about to make an important move.

"One thing's for sure," Sheridan said. "Even if anybody does know where we are, no one's going to follow us from here on out. I haven't seen anything yet that could keep up with a White Star on full burn."

───── *chapter 4* ─────

With the command for the jump from space to hyper-space, the *White Star*'s crew began the evolution that would take her from one piece of empty space to another.

Only this particular piece was not quite empty.

Sitting less than a mile from the *White Star* was a farseer 'bot. It was a small, rounded object, and it had gone unnoticed by the *White Star*'s detectors. The 'bot was small and glittering. It looked like a curved mass of quicksilver, and it reflected the *White Star*. It hung all by itself in the void of space, turning slowly to keep the Minbari craft in sight. The 'bot seemed alone and isolated, turning by itself with no sign of a guiding intelligence.

And yet, just *beneath* the surface of the object, a curious thing happened. Though the 'bot seemed solid, closer examination led to a brief, vertiginous tunneling effect.

This dizzying ride led to a sphere, small enough to be held in a man's hand. Obviously, it was remotely connected to the farseer 'bot.

A man was holding the sphere, a man whose face

was hidden in a hood, part of a cloak that muffled him from head to toe. The man was standing in a darkened room, its only source of light a powerglobe on the ground near where he sat, cross-legged.

In the glowing surface of the crystal sphere, the *White Star* picked up speed and vanished into a jump point that had opened in front of it. The man watched intently.

A voice behind the man with the sphere said, "Galen . . ."

Without turning around, the man with the probe responded. "I'm here."

"The Circle requires your presence."

Galen pushed back his hood and stood up. He was a tall young man, an Earther. "I'm busy," he said, his attention still on the probe.

"They know of your activities. You will come to them . . . or they will come to you. Either way, you *will* be called to account."

Galen moved uncomfortably, annoyed by the disturbance.

"We are all called to account, sooner or later," he said. "And to whom am I supposed to explain my behavior *this* time?"

"To everyone involved."

"Everyone? It must be a very large room."

"Galen," the voice said again. It was beginning to sound exasperated.

"All right, all right. Show me the way."

As he spoke, the room changed. Its sharp edges collapsed and everything around Galen became misty and indistinct. In the darkness, a line of small lights appeared on the ground in front of him. Looking up, he saw that the lights extended as far as he could see, seemingly to infinity.

He sighed. "The long road. But then, it's always the long road, isn't it? And you . . ." he said, speaking to the ship seen within the globe itself, "you may be called to account even sooner than you imagined."

He drew a black cloth out of his sleeve and covered the globe. When he pulled off the cloth, the probe was gone.

"Can we be on our way now?" the voice said, sounding quite testy.

—— chapter 5 ——

Lunch ended with a nice selection of liqueurs, brought over by a waiter in a white uniform. The White Star ships often carried exceptional cuisine, especially when they were transporting important passengers, and this selection was typical of the choices that could be offered.

Sheridan declined, since he wanted to keep his senses clear for the work ahead. Garibaldi, by his own instructions, was not offered the liqueur tray. He eyed it anyhow.

Picking their way through the normal clutter of equipment common to a recently commissioned ship, Sheridan and Garibaldi came to the bridge. A Minbari Ranger was seated at the main console, reading the instruments. He was taking great pains with his work, conscious that the eyes both of Garibaldi and the president of the Interstellar Alliance were on him. Biting his lip, he made tiny adjustments on the instruments until he had it just right. Then he got up and moved away.

Sheridan smiled at him and, with a by-your-leave gesture, slid into the chair.

"Mr. President, we've arrived at the rendezvous point," another member of the bridge crew announced.

"Good," Sheridan said. He settled down in front of the controls, looking them over quickly to reacquaint himself with their array. Then he said, "Lock in coordinates, prepare to jump to normal space . . . *Jump!*"

Everyone on the bridge had been waiting for that command. The response was little short of instantaneous. Ahead of the ship, a jump point formed. The *White Star* emerged into normal space.

Sheridan got up and relinquished the seat to the Ranger. He and Garibaldi strolled around the bridge. Through the window, Sheridan could see only the distant stars. But the *White Star* was rotating slowly.

The Minbari Ranger said, "We should be coming into visual range any time now."

"I hope this was worth it," Sheridan said. "I haven't seen anything on these ships since the initial designs came across my desk three years ago."

"Well," Garibaldi said with barely contained excitement, "if what I saw here last was any indication, I think you're gonna like this. I think you're gonna like this a lot." He looked through the window.

The *White Star* completed her rotation and was lined up with the object of their visit.

"There she blows!" Garibaldi said. "Our first two prototype destroyers."

The view had come up quickly. Now Sheridan could see a huge construction dock floating in space. It stretched out for hundreds of miles, longer than the average asteroid, its shiny metal painted a matte black. It was made of a heavy-gauge superalloy steel. You couldn't have built a dry dock this size on a planet with a normal gravity. The problems of inner bracing, needed to compensate for gravitational stress, would have been prohibitive.

The dock was an imposing sight with its gantries and cranes, its tractor-equipped working vehicles crawling like ants across its great spread of surface. It was a fit mark of imperial ambitions, the sort of thing men could do because they dared to do it. It was a thrilling sight. Sheridan watched eagerly as the *White Star* closed slowly toward the monolithic structure.

He couldn't make out too many details yet, but he could see the banners and bunting that Drake had ordered put up to mark the occasion. They looked a little strange in the vacuum of space, but at least they were there. And there was no mistaking the two finished ships moored alongside the dock.

The dock was huge, nearly a mile and a half long, and the two ships moored on either side of it were big, too. Bigger than most spacecraft Sheridan had worked with before. They were identical, and every inch bespoke power, making them seem as large as any man-made things found in space.

He sucked in his breath as he focused on them. The new ships were bold and startling in their sweeping lines and strange curves, with long, narrow bodies and sweeping fins—four on each ship—that reminded him of an eagle's wings. It was evident at a glance that they combined elements of Minbari and Human technology. There was even a touch of techno-organic Vorlon design. Each prototype was several times the size of a White Star. Their newly burnished hulls glittered in the construction lights lining either side of the huge dry dock. The two ships appeared to be identical in every way.

"The one on the left is *Excalibur*," Garibaldi said. "The other one is the *Victory*."

How do you fall in love with one of a set of twins? Sheridan's response was irrational and immediate. "I like the *Excalibur*," he said, looking at the ships. He couldn't say why he had chosen that one. Something about the name, perhaps, but also something that hinted that he might have found a new love.

"I thought you would," Garibaldi said, a smile playing across his face. "Let's go down and check her out."

There was a brief delay while the launch was taken out of storage where some fool had stowed her, then was set up on the launching platform. At last they were able to get aboard and aim for the *Excalibur*.

While a bosun maneuvered for a landing, they saw the small 'bots circling *Excalibur*, spotlighting it and finishing bits of cleanup work. Several tugs hovered above the big ships, like Lilliputians around twin Gullivers. On the dock, there were workers in white EVA suits cleaning up the final bits of debris from the dry dock's deck.

As they approached, Sheridan was even more impressed with *Excalibur*'s size. At a distance, it had been a marvel. Up close, it was overwhelming. But it was something more than that. It was also a dream come true, his long-held dream of a ship large enough and powerful enough to handle anything that came its way.

They came in through the main entry port. Within

Excalibur, there was the sharp smell of a new space-ship. There were new corridors to travel down, new detailing to admire, the whole sense of a new ship to take in.

John Sheridan was in his element. It was a throwback to the boy in him that nothing pleased him as much as a bright, complicated new toy. And if that toy, at a mile and a quarter in length, was longer than New York's World Trade Center back on Earth was high, all the better.

In a brightly lit corridor on their way to the bridge, Drake was waiting for them, with a Ranger honor guard lined up at attention. Sheridan's first impression was of a young man not quite sure of himself and trying to hide that fact by presenting a brave front.

Drake was not a bad-looking man, with a regular face and a high forehead. If a fault could be found, perhaps it was that his eyes didn't seem to quite focus on you. Perhaps because of this, his features seemed to betray a certain inner irresolution. Still, that might be no more than an unfortunate first impression. Sheridan had advised himself more than once not to rely too heavily on first impressions. Still . . .

"Mr. President, I'm Samuel Drake. It's an honor to meet you." His gaze took in Garibaldi. "Mr. Garibaldi, it's . . . good to see you again."

"I can tell," Garibaldi responded with more than a note of sarcasm.

Sheridan saw that there was no love lost between these two. Drake seemed a pleasant enough individual. Garibaldi was his usual surly self. Was there a reason behind his animosity toward Drake? Sheridan knew he'd find out soon enough.

Meanwhile, trying to inspire at least a fragile peace between these two, Sheridan said, "So let's begin the tour, shall we?" Setting the example, he led the way down the corridor.

Drake talked as they went along. His speech was somewhat hurried, and gave further evidence of his desire to please.

He led them from one part of the ship to another, past the mess hall, the neat but cramped living quarters, the flight bay for landing ships, a recreation room with a large vaulted ceiling. It was all neat, obviously in pristine working order, ready for use. Drake commented all of the way, and he seemed less interested in pointing out the ship's good qualities than in complaining about everything that had gone wrong, all of it someone else's fault.

"So far, we've only been able to get the gravitetic propulsion system to provide a workable gravity of slightly less than one G. After three months of trying, we've decided to declare victory and leave it there."

"Probably better for everyone than a full G anyway," Sheridan said.

"I agree," Drake said. He seemed pleased and a little surprised that Sheridan was siding with him. Sheridan's continuing diagnosis was that Drake was suffering from too much exposure to Mr. Garibaldi.

During one part of the tour, Drake stopped, and in a somewhat formal manner said, "Incidentally, sir, I want to thank you for bringing me aboard. It's not easy for Mars-born citizens to get work on major Earth contracts."

"Not a problem," Sheridan said. "I don't have much

patience with that kind of bias. Under the Alliance, Mars-born and Earth naturals are entitled to equal opportunities. Besides, you came highly recommended."

Garibaldi's expression said, "I could tell you a thing or two about people who come highly recommended." But he didn't say anything. Not then.

They moved into the area of the bridge, passing side offices and compartments. The ship was very spacious, with an amount of room previously unknown in Earth spaceship design. There were ladders and elevators at many locations. Sheridan knew he'd have to familiarize himself with the entire layout soon. And he was going to love every minute of it.

The bridge was different from what Sheridan had been expecting, and he commented on this to Drake.

Drake explained, "We decided on a nonstandard bridge configuration, based on the submarine model. Linear instead of circular. From the captain's chair it's a straight throw back and across to the other compartments."

There were several workers on the bridge. Final touches were still being put in place. Some workers were laying cable. Others were fitting some of the final paneling.

Drake ticked off what they were seeing. "Map room ... conference room ... navigation and helm controls ... com system ... weapons. We designed the controls along EarthForce lines to make them easier for us to deal with. The system's very intuitive; you can run it almost like any other ship. It's what's inside that matters."

"How does she handle?" Sheridan asked.

He could tell by Garibaldi's expression that he had stumbled, innocently enough, onto a sore spot.

"We . . . don't actually know," Drake said. "We wanted to wait until you got here and she was completely fitted out."

Sheridan frowned. "Mr. Drake, don't you think you should find out whether or not she could go anywhere before you spend a lot of time polishing the chrome? What if this new propulsion system doesn't work?"

"All the tests have indicated—"

Just then, Drake's wrist link *bleep*ed. He touched it. "Yes?"

They could all hear an officer's voice saying, "Message for President Sheridan on StellarCom. It's from Delenn."

Drake turned his attention to Sheridan and said, "You can take it in the conference room, Mr. President."

Sheridan nodded. "I think I know the way." He left the bridge.

As he did so, Garibaldi found a chair and sat down. His movements were slow, purposeful, contained. He fixed Drake with a baleful eye.

"Drake, did I, or did I not, tell you to take this thing out at least once before we got here? Did I, or did I not, introduce you to the theory of 'it doesn't have to be perfect, let's just see if it works'?"

"Yes, but—"

"Then perhaps it's time I introduced you to a new theory. It's called 'shut up and do what I tell you.' Now ease her out of spacedock."

Drake looked like he had another excuse to make.

But one glance at Garibaldi's compressed lips and slitted eyes changed his mind.

"Yes, sir."

Garibaldi said to Drake, "Do it."

Drake turned to the Ranger at the navigation controls. "Cast off ties, prepare to ease her away from spacedock."

"Aye, sir," the navigation officer said.

"Fire up!" Drake said.

The navigation officer worked quickly with his controls. On the dry dock, a series of flashing lights warned the workers to get under cover—just in case. The *Excalibur* slowly drifted away from the steel side of the dry dock, moving with the sleepwalking pace of a dormant giant. There was a deep roar as the engines fired up . . . followed almost immediately by a whine as they powered down. The next sound was that of a *pooph*, as though the engines were laughing at them. Finally, a loud clank like a hundred-yard-long wrench hitting the floor of the ship's hull.

Garibaldi had elected not to explode with anger at the moment, though you could see it was difficult for him. In a rigidly controlled voice, he said, "Drake, was that a problem?"

Drake, tight-lipped with mortification, muttered, "So it would seem. Sir!"

Mr. Garibaldi's expression was not a pleasant one to behold.

—— chapter 6 ——

After Garibaldi left, Drake gave the necessary orders and returned to the personal quarters he had allotted to himself on the spacedock. There he threw himself into the worn swivel chair that served him for an armchair. He wore an expression of petulance. That ass, Garibaldi! What gave him the right? Then his expression turned to one of concern. Every delay might lead to a closer examination of the work—of *his* work. That could spell disaster . . .

The room was spartan, like all the living quarters on that colossal structure, but Drake had fixed it up with a few personal touches. On the wall above his computer was his framed diploma from MUT, the Martian University of Technology. It was a place he had cordially detested, not least for its pretensions to elitism—as if anything on Mars could be considered elite!

And what was good on Mars counted for next to nothing on Earth. Drake had graduated third in his class of 475. On Mars, that was superb. On Earth, his degree was considered the equivalent of a barely passing grade at a not very good community college.

On the table, beside his computer, was a set of old

dice, yellowed, their edges rounded. They had belonged to his father. Morton G. Drake had gambled with them, and with dice very much like them, in all the gambling halls and casinos of Mars. There were few libraries on Mars, but there were a surprising number of casinos. His father had been in and out of every one of them, and had converted his construction engineer's salary into debts that had mounted astronomically as he had kept trying to get even. Until he finally blew his brains out one especially disastrous night. He had been forty-three years old.

Drake had inherited one thing from his father—his passion. But in Drake's case, that passion was for precision, *not* for risk-taking. Drake never gambled, never took chances. And now, here was Mr. High-and-Mighty Garibaldi, reaming him out for not going out on a limb with the biggest ship in creation. Calling him Pussyfoot and other, much worse names. It was as though Garibaldi was telling him he could use a few of his father's gambler's genes.

So Garibaldi thought Drake wasn't a gambler, eh? Well, Garibaldi would be surprised to learn that Drake could, indeed, take a risk when the odds were big enough. He *was* taking a chance. A big one. And Mr. Garibaldi soon would learn of it, to his regret.

Near the dice sat a framed photograph of his mother, a nice-looking, faded woman with short, dark hair. She had survived Drake's father by only three years. Silicosis had taken her away—the dubious gift of the air outlet tubes that blew dust from the mine where she had worked for twenty years as a bookkeeper. Not that he could ever prove the connection. Not that the company would ever admit to even a part of the responsibility.

Drake sighed and wished he had something to drink. His nerves were frayed from Garibaldi's abrasive tirade. Then he noticed his computer was blinking and realized that he had E-mail. His expression brightened. He called it up at once.

It was from Cora. Who else would write to him?

"Dear Samuel," she wrote, "I've been able to do it at last! I'm coming to your famous dry dock on the next ship leaving Babylon 5. They want me to look into the oxygen-regenerating plant array we've set up there. I'm so excited! Imagine it, me, a Holyoke girl with a minor degree in extraterrestrial biology, getting a chance on a big job like this! Oh, my work won't be much more than checking numbers off a clipboard—no great skill required!—but it's a beginning!

"It will be so nice to see you again. I was greatly impressed by our talk, that time you visited B5. And your views on Earth-Martian politics and the unfairness shown by Earth people toward the Martian-born gave me a lot to think about.

"See you soon. Yours, Cora."

Drake looked away from the letter and tried to calm himself. But there was nothing he could do about the waves of joy that seemed to burst over his head. And nothing he wanted to do. Cora was coming to see him! This was the most wonderful news in the world.

That a girl like Cora—an Earth girl, tall, slender, blond, educated, of a good family—a *patrician*!—was crossing empty space to see him had to mean something. She didn't say so in her E-mail, but that was because she was a formal person. Unless he mistook the signs, her visit meant that she felt something for him, just as he loved her.

Of course, he had never told her so. And she didn't say anything to that effect outright. But he was sure he could read the signs, sure she reciprocated his own feelings. And now she was coming to the spacedock!

He laughed, and his face became almost handsome. He'd reveal his feelings to her this time. She would see how right they were for each other. She would agree to marry him. And then he'd put the nightmare behind him.

But was that still possible? Did he have the time to undo the strange nightmare of the past months, the long slide that had begun in a Martian bar when he'd gone on leave? There, he'd actually found someone—a perfect stranger—who had listened to him, sympathized with his grievances. A few drinks, and Drake had actually found himself offered riches, and a chance at revenge for the indignities heaped upon him by those snotty Earth types.

His face flushed with panic as he thought about it now. Where had all his caution gone, his lifetime of weighing one thing against another? Like a fool he had listened to the stranger's ideas and agreed with the justice of them. These Earth people thought they owned all creation and everything in it! They'd soon see! It had been such a relief to say what he felt, to someone who seemed to understand.

But now he was trapped.

Or was he?

It still wasn't too late to back out. He could get out of

it. He hadn't committed himself irrevocably, not yet. He was a prominent person; they couldn't touch him if he changed his mind. They wouldn't dare.

He heaved a long, shuddering sigh. He could end all this. With Cora at his side, anything was possible.

── chapter 7 ──

A call from Delenn was such a pleasant thing to look forward to. Sheridan was surprised. They hadn't planned to talk for another few days. Still, it was a welcome treat.

Sheridan strode down the corridor leading from the bridge to the interior parts of the ship. He was sure of his direction, but hadn't counted on the size of the vessel. It took a lot longer to get from point to point on *Excalibur* than it did on a White Star. The walk was pleasant enough, down a wide corridor that seemed to dip slightly downward as he walked on it. The lighting was even, monotonous, hypnotic. He thought it might be a good idea to do something more dramatic with it. This evenly lit corridor, which gave the sensation that you were traveling into the depths of a dream, was almost hypnotic to the senses. Some sounds would also be good here. Help to wake people up!

Still, that was a minor point. So far, he approved of the ship's layout. It showed good common sense. He had to congratulate Drake on that.

He found his way without difficulty to the conference room. It was large and pleasantly lit, with con-

trasting pastel wall colors and rug. It had the good
smell of a new ship about it. Inside, there was a long
light-colored table, with six chairs around it. Near the
far wall was a small table with a pot of steaming coffee
ready for him. Sheridan smiled. He was sure Garibaldi
had thought of this detail.

He poured himself a cup of coffee, sipped it appre-
ciatively for a moment, and went to the chair at the
head of the table, next to a video monitor with its ready
light blinking.

Sheridan spoke. "You have a message for me?"

The computer monitor's voice replied, "Message received, President Sheridan. Ready to display."

"Good, let's see it," Sheridan said, and he leaned forward toward the screen.

The monitor came to life in a series of vivid swirling
colors. That was strange. Sheridan couldn't remember
ever seeing anything like it. *Excalibur* must be using
new software, he thought. The swirling colors changed
into interlocking shapes, turning, twirling, coalescing
and separating again. No data was coming through, no
printout, not even an explanatory voice-over. But Sheridan found that he wasn't impatient. It was strangely
soothing just sitting in front of this glowing screen, relaxed, watching the changing shapes and colors. Like
watching a dream. Funny he should think of that . . .

He watched the display, and he felt slowed down and
content. Tension that he hadn't even been aware of
seemed to be draining from his muscles. He sat there,
perfectly relaxed, the cup of coffee cooling beside him,
forgotten, and watched the swirling shapes.

Even when the display went off he was still perfectly at ease, and in no hurry to move.

Garibaldi was nervous and impatient. Ten minutes seemed long enough to him for the president to receive his message and get back to the bridge. He waited another five minutes. No message came from the conference room, even though it was connected to the bridge. Faint alarm bells went off in Garibaldi's mind. He was sure nothing was wrong . . . but still . . .

He got up and hurried down the corridor to the conference room.

The door was closed. Protocol demanded that he wait until Sheridan summoned him. His own built-in sense of urgency disagreed. He pressed his ear against the door and tried to hear what was going on. He couldn't make out a sound.

He straightened and began pacing, trying to decide what to do. He was not happy about this at all. He walked up and down outside the door, glancing frequently at his watch. He had other stuff on *Excalibur* to show to Sheridan, and he knew the president was eager to see it all. So what was he doing, staying in there so long? This wasn't like Sheridan at all. He had never been a man to waste time on personal communications during an official transmission. Not even with Delenn. Why was this changing now?

He looked again at his watch. Sheridan had been in there for twenty minutes easy, maybe longer. It was unthinkable for Garibaldi to interrupt, but he suspected that something was going wrong. It was his habit to follow his suspicions. But still he hung back.

When nearly half an hour had passed, Garibaldi was at last convinced enough that something was going on. He defied the rules of privacy, opened the door, and poked his head in.

"Mr. President, are you okay?"

Sheridan, seated in a relaxed posture in front of the console, looked up with a smile. "Why shouldn't I be okay?" he asked.

"Because you've been in there almost half an hour."

"That's not possible," Sheridan said. He shook his head, though, as if to clear out the cobwebs. "I just got here. The message was scrambled. Gibberish. Drake hasn't installed new software, has he?"

Garibaldi shook his head.

"Then it must be some kind of interference."

"You stayed looking at gibberish for twenty minutes? Hell, if you're gonna do that, you might as well come by my place sometime, and I'll show you some twentieth-century television."

Sheridan didn't seem to find the remark funny. At least, he didn't smile. The president had looked fine before the transmission. But now Garibaldi saw that he suddenly seemed tired, played out. There were lines of strain around his eyes, a tension to his lips.

Seeing this, Garibaldi decided the rest of the tour could wait.

"Listen," Garibaldi said, "Drake still has a few bugs to work out. Nothing serious, but it'll take a while. Get some rest, we'll finish the tour later."

"Fine," Sheridan said. "Good idea. Guess I'm more tired than I thought."

Garibaldi left the conference room and shut the door

gently. Drake had come up from the bridge and was looking uneasy.

"Is something wrong?" he asked. "Is the president all right? I certainly hope there's nothing—"

"The president is fine," Garibaldi said flatly. "There's someone else you should be worrying about."

"Who?"

"That's you," Garibaldi said. "Now we're gonna figure out a way to move this thing." His glance took in the ship. "Or you're going to go outside and push."

"I'll get right on it!" Drake hurried away.

Garibaldi nodded at the retreating figure, and mused to himself, "Things were so much easier on Babylon 5."

──── chapter 8 ────

On Babylon 5 at this point in time, a line of new arrivals had reached customs and was moving slowly through the scanners. Zack Allan was standing a little ways back at his station, watching them. He saw that it was the usual ragtag bunch that drifted into Babylon 5 from all over the galaxy. There were Humans and aliens from a dozen different worlds. They were not a well-dressed bunch, although most of them were wearing what passed for their best back where they came from. Their clothing looked more than a little odd here. As usual, there were some from worlds Zack couldn't identify.

As security chief, one of Zack's prime areas of interest was this customs line. When trouble came to Babylon 5, this was its typical entry point, among these people seeking work or fun or trouble or adventure on this smallest of civilized worlds.

Babylon 5 was a self-sustaining civilization just over five miles long and holding roughly 250,000 persons. It was a place of commerce and peace in a neutral territory and, as such, had become a focal point for most of the intelligent races of the galaxy. Some of those who were entering now were on their way to somewhere else, but those who were staying always managed to keep things interesting.

This woman coming into the inspection area now was worth a second look. She was humanoid, though not Human. Small but striking, just over five feet tall, golden-eyed, dressed in dark leathers and bright, flexible metals. She had wild, raven hair that fell down over her shoulders and a to-hell-with-you air about her that was intriguing, to say the least.

Her papers said she was Dureena Nafeel. Home planet, Zander Prime. Zack thought he had heard that name before, but he couldn't place it. There were so many planets! Maybe he'd look it up later when he had some free time.

Dureena took long strides through the scanners. A monitor near Zack read WEAPONS VIOLATION. Zack stepped forward toward her.

"Ma'am? Can I see you over here?"

He escorted her to a private area near customs.

"What's the matter?" Dureena asked with a touch of defiance in her voice.

"I guess you didn't read the postings outside," Zack said. "Babylon 5 has a strict weapons policy. Now, either give me whatever you're carrying, or I'll have to ask you to leave the station."

She studied him with all the interest she'd give to a bug, then pulled a long-bladed knife from her belt, handed it to him hilt-first, and started to move away.

Zack, still keeping his voice pleasant, said, "All of it. You can pick it up when you leave."

The woman looked from him to the guards, as

though assessing how much trouble it would be to take them out. She seemed to think it wouldn't be difficult at all, but decided it would stir up too much trouble. This was neither the time nor the place.

There, in front of Zack's astonished eyes, she pulled a short sword from a hiding place behind her back, another blade from her belt. With a flick of the wrist she produced a wickedly curved knife from each boot, a garrote from around her waist . . . Before she was done, nearly a dozen weapons, exotic and lethal, had been added to the collection on the countertop.

"That's it," she said with finality.

"Thanks a lot," Zack replied.

"Can I go now?"

"Be my guest."

She went through the customs barrier, then stopped, apparently bewildered by the proliferation of corridors and levels that lay ahead of her. Near her, two small humanoids were playing a game with colored bones. A panatos salesman was offering his small, warm buns. Passing close by were oddly assorted couples, most notably a gigantic woman in a garish green shift paired with a very small man in a simulated leopard-skin jumpsuit. Where did *that* duo come from?

There was a babble of conversation covering the whole auditory range, from bass grumblings to high-pitched twitters and squeaks. And the colors! Bright, flashing, constantly shifting. It was difficult to make out shapes; everything became a pandemonium of coalescing images.

And where was she supposed to go in all this?

She turned to Zack. "Where do the lost people go?"

"Who?" Zack said.

"The forgotten. The castoffs. The neglected. The lost people."

Zack nodded in understanding. "Down Below. Brown Sector."

With the barest nod of her head in acknowledgment, Dureena strode off. Zack watched her go, wondering if this one was going to be trouble.

He wasn't the only one watching Dureena on the day of her arrival.

— chapter 9 —

On *Excalibur*, Sheridan walked down the long, curving, evenly lit corridor looking for an empty sleeping cubicle. There were plenty of them: *Excalibur* was still an empty ship, without her complement of soldiers aboard. He could have any room he cared to take, or any ten of them, for that matter. They were all the same, anyhow, without any personal touches yet.

"I guess this'll do as well as any other," Sheridan said to himself, choosing one of the sleeping cubicles at random. It was comforting to him, the simplicity of the small, rectangular space. There was nothing in it but a bunk bed, a desk, a StellarCom monitor, and two chairs. There was an adjoining bathroom, and the whole thing was lit by a powerglobe, putting out its even, shadowless glow.

Sheridan threw himself onto the bed, boots and all. "Dim," he said, and the powerglobe turned the room to dusk.

He could think of a dozen things he ought to do before going to sleep. Paramount among them were taking off his boots, undressing, taking a shower. But he was too tired to do any of them. He couldn't remember when he'd last felt such a bone-deep fatigue.

He lay there on the bed, looking at the pastel ceiling, thinking vague thoughts, and sleep came to him. With it came a dream. Or was it a dream?

He was standing on rocky, uneven ground, and it was dark. A wind was blowing, and he could feel a gritty dust in the air. The area was fitfully illuminated by fires burning in the immense landscape that stretched around him on all sides.

Everything was lava and scorched rock. There wasn't a tree or any green thing in sight. Turning, he saw, at a distance, the ruined crater of a city silhouetted black against the charcoal-gray sky. Fires were burning in the city, too, and columns of smoke rose into the sky.

He sensed that this was what his recent dreams had been about. But this time, he knew he would remember.

Sheridan could also sense that this had once been a beautiful place. Even in ruins, the city showed signs of a former nobility. Even at this distance, he could see there were minarets and spires lying in the streets like the bodies of fallen giants, and they were mixed with the remains of a classical, unearthly sculpture, giant heads and torsos lying in the rubble-choked streets. This had been a place devoted to the arts.

Lightning flashed in the sky, double and triple forked, revealing a devastated landscape as far as the eye could see. Sheridan didn't need a guided tour to know that all this world was dead, ravaged, bereft of life, even vegetable life, even algae. Somehow, he knew. Something or someone had really done a job on this world, devouring the forests, drying up the seas, sweeping away the cities and other Human habitations.

He turned slowly, looking at all this in sorrow and slowly mounting anger. And at the same time he was wondering, *Where the hell am I? What's going on here?*

As if in answer to his thoughts, a voice came out of the darkness and said, "Do you hear that?"

Sheridan turned quickly in the direction of the voice. He could just make out a robed figure squatting on the ground beside the cliff face. The man's face was concealed behind a hood. He was bent over, scratching on the ground with a stick.

"Who the hell are you?" Sheridan demanded.

"I am called Galen," he answered. Then, "Do you hear it?"

"Hear what?"

"Listen," Galen said.

"I don't hear anything," Sheridan said.

"Exactly. No birds, no animals, no machines, no voices. And no insects, or starships, or music. Only the wind. You are hearing the sound of a dead world. A murdered world."

"Was there an attack?" Sheridan asked.

"Nothing so grand as that. It was a test. Can you imagine that? All this, just for a test!"

Sheridan shook his head slowly. What in hell was going on? He was aboard *Excalibur*. He was asleep!

He shook his head slowly. "This is a dream."

"No," Galen said. "Not a dream. A nightmare. And if sometimes dreams come true, then what of our nightmares?"

"Who are you?" Sheridan asked.

"A friend. I called to you earlier." Galen pushed back his cowl, revealing a square, good-looking face with strong features. He was dark-eyed, hairless save for his brows, and he had the disciplined look of a monk or acolyte. His face at present showed concern, but Sheridan thought he could see the possibilities of a sly humor beneath that.

With a hint of embarrassment, Galen said, "That message from Delenn . . . that was me. I apologize for the deception. But a connection was necessary for the electron incantation."

Before Sheridan could speak, he heard a deep, distant, massive humming noise. He identified it at once as the sound of a fleet of spaceships, approaching, but still a long way away.

Sheridan said, "I thought you said this world was dead."

"It is. The killers are coming back to check on their handiwork. We should go. They probably can't pick up on my probe, but there's no point in risking it."

He looked at Sheridan—an electrifying look. "*Remember* what you have seen."

The humming sound increased and Sheridan looked toward the sky. He thought he saw something moving through the clouds—something dark and massive and made of strange angles—a huge spaceship of some kind . . .

When he looked down again, Galen was gone.

"There were some things I wanted to ask him," Sheridan said ruefully.

He looked at the spot where Galen had been. The ground was marked where he had been digging with his stick. It looked like letters. Sheridan walked around to where Galen had been squatting. He could read what Galen had scratched in the dirt. Words. *Daltron 7.*

The name of a planet, most likely. But Sheridan didn't think he had ever heard of a world by that name.

He looked up again as the humming sound increased. He had the impression that the massive spaceship was coming closer.

He searched the sky, trying to make out its shape. And found he was looking at the pastel ceiling above his bunk bed aboard *Excalibur*.

He sat up, startled. From the nearby window, he could see that *Excalibur* was slowly moving away from the spacedock. To one side he could see the space tugs that were towing the big ship out.

"Guess they got it fixed," Sheridan said aloud.

He took the time now to shower and shave. Then he poured himself a coffee from a carafe and sat down to think things over.

He knew that something amazing had happened to him, but he didn't know what it was or what it meant. No doubt the meaning of what he had seen would be revealed to him in the fullness of time. His impatient spirit rebelled against that thought. He wanted the answers now, but there was no way he could get them. Although it didn't suit his nature, he had to be patient.

For a moment Sheridan considered the possibility that his blackouts might be the result of job pressure—the office of the presidency finally taking its toll. His position was demanding, and he took his duty very seriously. The lives of countless individuals required that he do so. It had been that way for five years.

Years. How many of those did he have remaining? How many had he left behind, on Z'ha'dum? That was another source of pressure—the ticking of the clock. Twenty years and counting.

This isn't doing anyone any good, he mused. *I know what I've seen, and ignoring it won't get me anywhere.* Best to get back to work. The full truth would reveal itself in due course.

He went up to the bridge. Garibaldi was sitting in the captain's chair. He got up when Sheridan came in. Drake was standing nearby. The man didn't seem to know what to do with his hands. He was plucking nervously at a button on his uniform, quite unconscious of what he was doing.

Drake said, "I had to call up those tugs at pretty short notice. We could really use a few more."

Garibaldi shrugged unsympathetically. "It ain't pretty, but at least it'll get us out to the firing range. You get to live another ten minutes, Drake."

Drake stared at Garibaldi's face: blank, hostile, sardonic. How he hated the man! But there was nothing he could do about it yet. He forced his own face into a formal mask of acceptance. He was going to have to take this for a little longer.

"Yes, sir," Drake said in a formal tone. "Thank you, sir."

—— *chapter 10* ——

Although she'd heard of this place even before she had arrived on Babylon 5, Dureena still found Down Below astonishing, a cacophony of chaos—especially after the clean, modernistic look of the customs area. Going through there had been like moving through a dream of a better world, all of it bright and clean and shiny.

But Down Below was a different sort of a vision—a glimpse of what a place comes to look like when no one pays any attention to it, and when it's occupied by a floating population that doesn't care how they live.

She was in a crowded, industrial-looking area, something like a warehouse district in some ancient Earth city. A line of cars rattled by on overhead rails, throwing down showers of sparks. Machinery, disused and abandoned, lay piled against the walls or out in the rudimentary streets that wove, seemingly in haphazard, patternless lines, through the area. The air was warm, moist, hazy, with a tang of machine oil and chemicals. Steam oozed from fittings on pipes long past their time of inspection.

There were people passing through this area, or just

hanging out; people in ragged, shapeless clothing, warming their hands over heat barrels, killing time while time slowly killed them. Dureena noticed representatives of half the races of the galaxy, not all of them humanoid. Most of them were air-breathers, although a few wore respirating equipment to let them function here in this common area before returning to the more congenial atmospheric mixes of their own special sectors. But most of them seemed able to function in B5's oxygen atmosphere.

Dureena glided through the populace, trying not to call attention to herself—though she was aware that her costume stood out too much in this place, and wished she'd brought along something more appropriate.

Despite the amazing variety of beings found there— each wearing his or her own native garb—many of the denizens of Down Below seemed to possess some intuitive sense that told them when someone new had arrived. Since she was the only survivor of Zander Prime, she couldn't help but stand out in the crowd. To Dureena, it seemed as though all eyes had turned her way.

Nonetheless, she was trying to act as if she had always lived here, a wised-up citizen of this place. And so she moved through the multicolored, fantastically arrayed crowd of the lost people of Down Below, looking for she knew not what, yet somehow aware that this was the end of the line, for the moment.

Down Below! It was said that your nerves and your bad luck brought you here, far from whatever world you originated in. And here you ran out of your last vestiges of luck, or nerve, or both, and settled into the scruffy, comfortable life of scuffling along, taking it one day at a time, getting by, and not even noticing that the sands of your life were running out of the huge hourglass that marked each sentient creature's days and hours.

There were rules of behavior, even in a place like this. *Especially* in a place like this. Dureena picked them up intuitively. The people of Down Below minded their own business. Many of them just liked to drift along in their own dreams, content to mind their own concerns, ignorant of the greater life that pulsed around them.

But not everyone could afford to be so out of it. Nor did everyone want to. Many, rich and poor, had a living that had to be won each day. They all had to keep their eyes open for what came up, the unexpected opportunity or unprecedented disaster, and find a way to put it to good use. Any object, carelessly lost or discarded or stolen, might be sold, because there was a market here for just about everything.

But if you couldn't find something to sell, there was always the possibility of latching onto some person new to Down Below and unfamiliar with its ways. Using who or what you found helped you get by another day, or maybe even another year, if you hit it lucky.

Hycher Vlast was thinking such thoughts as he idled beside a heat barrel. He was a short, long-nosed, weasel-faced man with small darting eyes. A scar along his jawline bespoke an encounter with someone even less amiable than himself. Three healing scratches on his face gave evidence of his relationship to the opposite sex.

Vlast was a scavenger who aspired to be something greater—a conspirator, perhaps. He had managed to get a good free meal the previous night—a consignment of old meats from the throwaways of the Eddisto, one of the newer restaurants. He had begged his dinner from Med, the busboy, whose vegetarian constitution had no use for it, and who owed Vlast a favor.

Vlast didn't have much money on him. But he did have his eyes open. And when he saw the compact, golden-skinned woman, he sensed that he had come upon an opportunity.

She was a newcomer. He could tell this by her strangely alien features, and the way she tried to blend in with the crowd. Her clothing alone would have given her away as a new arrival. She had on the sort of outfit a fighting man or woman would wear. Was she looking for bodyguard work? There was no fighting down here, unless you counted the occasional drunken scuffle and, of course, the assassin's dagger in the dark.

But since she was raw, and ignorant of Down Below's ways, she had to be gullible, he reasoned. Here was a rich opportunity for Vlast.

Nonchalantly, he began walking behind her, keeping a good distance to prevent being noticed. There was no need for following too closely, anyhow: she wasn't going anywhere. She could run, but she could not hide. There was no place she could get to here where Vlast could not find her. In his five years in Down Below, Vlast had learned every twist and turn of the place, every hidey-hole, every closet and cupboard.

The woman had a casual air about her that Vlast figured must be feigned. She was looking for something, he was sure of that. And who better than he to help her find it? For a price, of course. Always for a price.

She stopped, and he stopped, too. Something had attracted her attention. And now she was moving again, more surely now, into a tangle where five corridors met.

Vlast hurried after her, moving as quickly as his stubby legs would take him, his ragged coat floating out behind him.

Into the tangle of streets. Five directions to choose from. No sign of the woman in any of them.

Damn it! What was the use of knowing all of Down Below if you didn't know what path your quarry had taken through it?

He calmed himself. She'd had beginner's luck, eluding him that way. He'd find her. There was no place for her to go.

—— *chapter 11* ——

When Dureena had entered Down Below, she'd had no idea where she was going. How could she? It was the first time she'd seen this place. The folks around here didn't furnish any street maps, and there certainly were no street signs. Nor was she about to ask directions from any of the people in the area, who, to say the least, looked very strange.

Maybe she didn't know where she was going, but she knew what she was looking for.

The organization to which she belonged was clandestine, secret, illegal, but very far-ranging. They had branches everywhere, on all planets where civilized beings assembled. She was sure she'd find some sign of them here.

She moved at random through a howling metal wilderness of coiling and intersecting corridors running off at bewildering angles. Steam, leaking out of vents and loosened pipe fittings, furnished spooky effects, making the denizens of this place indistinct. They moved through the warm fog like ghosts of themselves.

The people she passed seemed to come from all corners of the universe. Only a few of them were Humans, and they were not the best-looking examples of that species. Many of them looked like they had been damaged in transit, or maybe they'd been malformed to begin with. And the aliens were no better. A great number were clad in cast-off bits of native costume—as was Dureena herself—but they carried it off less tastefully, she thought. She couldn't identify most of the races. There were a few good-looking red-skinned ones, tall and with delicate features. They could almost be Human. But if so, why were they invariably in consort with a short, scaly bald species with long antennae on their foreheads? Symbiotes? Or sheer chance? There were mysteries here that would take a lot of time to clear up.

She went by several little food markets, the goods spread out on the sidewalk. Did people actually eat that stuff? A little farther on, she passed a fast-food stall selling a meat-filled bun that reminded her of klashpies, a delicacy of her native region—back when she'd had a native region. She was tempted to sample one, but decided to check it out later. There was no telling what they might put into those buns. And money was a problem, though, she hoped, not for long.

The sector was crowded, especially where several corridors intersected, forming open spaces where people could hang out and talk. In one of the open areas she saw two dancers, of a species she couldn't immediately identify, dancing to the sounds of a drum and fife played by two vaguely Human-looking people. She stopped for a moment to watch, and felt someone come up behind her.

"Hello, little lady," a voice said. She turned. It was a Dipsha, a species she'd rarely encountered. This one was leering at her. He was wearing a ridiculous purple velvet cap that she supposed was to make him attractive.

"What do you want?" Dureena asked doubtfully.

"Fun," the Dipsha said. "Frolicsome fun. You and me together. In a place I know. I pay good."

"Get lost," Dureena said.

The Dipsha looked like he wanted to take offense at the remark, but, noting Dureena's aggressive readiness, he controlled himself and moved away.

He was the first of the people on the make, but not the last. Several other men, or at least males of whatever species they were from, indicated that they'd be happy to make her acquaintance. Some of them seemed ready to force their attentions on her, but something about her look—the taut, well-conditioned look of a person accustomed to fighting—put them off, and they spared her their importunities. Dureena had a look that said, I am not to be taken lightly.

She continued walking, her gaze roving the surfaces of her new home, looking for a familiar sign. But when one came, she almost missed it.

She saw just the barest indication of a swirl of paint, half-hidden behind a decaying poster. Pushing it aside, Dureena saw an odd-shaped glyph painted on the wall in red and violet. It was circular, its circumference made up of short, curving lines that did not join. There was a twist on one side of the glyph. It looked like an afterthought, but Dureena knew it indicated a direction. She went the way it pointed, down another corridor, and then she climbed up a series of stanchions set into the wall.

—— chapter 12 ——

Down Below was all eyes. Someone was watching Dureena's moves. This time it wasn't Vlast; for the moment, he had been left behind, baffled. The person watching her was named Rolf.

Rolf was a large, imposing man, wearing ragged clothes that might once upon a time have been rather fine. He was bald-headed, imperious in his movements, yet with a feline quality about him that let him dissolve into a crowd. He had a gift for being unobtrusive, almost invisible.

If Dureena had noticed him, which she did not, she would have envied his ability to appear not to be there. If there was one thing she was having trouble with on Babylon 5, it was blending in with the crowd. She was highly skilled at what she did, but her distinctly alien features and her clothing, which was splendid and barbaric, called far too much attention to her.

Rolf was observing all this, and he noted that the lady's feisty quality was not a good trait in this place. Many fierce people had come to Down Below, and sooner or later they had all learned that there was always someone fiercer, stronger, more feral. It was a valuable lesson, if one could learn it and remain alive.

Dureena turned a corner and found another marker on a wall, the same design as before, only this time the pointer indicated a direction straight up. The only obvious way was through an open grate, too high to jump for. She found a couple of pipes set into the wall, climbed, then pulled herself into the grate.

She was in an air duct, a square pipe that sloped upward at a steep angle. Setting her feet, she made her way through it, finding handholds, slithering snake-like, around one bend and then another, until at last she came to an egress that dropped her in a wholly unfamiliar area.

Cautiously, she poked her head out. She was still in Down Below—that much was clear—in a place filled with battered garbage cans and discarded boxes. There seemed to be no one around. She pulled herself out. Then she looked around again—and froze.

Someone was pressing a gun to the back of her head.

Whoever could get behind her that way was good—very good. She was about to congratulate him on his stealth. But the man spoke first.

"Good night," Rolf said. And he coldcocked her with the gun butt.

Coming out of unconsciousness was not what Dureena had expected. She was in a place that wasn't at all like Babylon 5, didn't seem to be in or on Babylon 5. She was lying on frozen ground, in a cold place plagued by high winds and swirling dust.

But how could that be? Down Below had been

steamy, sweaty, pungent with the odorous effluvia of its many inhabitants.

Where was she?

Dureena opened her eyes, blinked, and scrambled to her feet.

She was on a gigantic tumbled landscape of bare, twisted rock and shining black solidified lava. She was near a cliff wall that rose high and sheer above her. Standing back, she could see broken walls and tumbled buildings where a city had once stood.

Clouds roiled in the nighttime sky, and flashes of forked lightning lit up the scene in sepulchral flashes.

It was a place she thought she remembered.

"Oh, no!" Dureena gasped. "I can't be back . . . I can't . . ."

"Can't you?" a voice asked.

She turned. A tall man in a uniform was smiling at her. Sheridan! She had memorized his face; she would know him anywhere! The detested Earther, author of all her woes! Her reaction was immediate, lethal. She launched herself at him, prepared to maim, kill, destroy this hated enemy whom she had never met, but knew very well.

Her charge carried her right through him, and his image rippled as she came out the other side and rolled in the dirt.

It had been nothing but an image, with nothing substantial about it.

She turned to face it again, but now the image had changed. Instead of Sheridan, it was a Drakh, its hideous face grinning at her in a sneer of triumph.

She tensed herself to charge again. But the Drakh

was holding something in his hand, stretching it out toward her. In his open hand was a tiny Milky Way galaxy.

As she watched, his fingers closed around it. The light from the galaxy briefly bled through his fingers, and then went dark.

And then the image of the Drakh was gone. And a voice was speaking to her.

"This is not your world, Dureena Nafeel. But it shared a common fate."

She turned, and found a cloaked young man standing behind her.

"I am called Galen," the man said. He held up his hand as she tensed, prepared to attack again. "When the time comes to choose your target, be sure to pick the right one. Because you will get only one shot."

She stared at him, trying to make sense of his words, trying to grasp the situation. Then the land shook beneath her and she was knocked to the ground.

When she opened her eyes again, she was back on Babylon 5, in Down Below. Her hands were manacled. And there was a circle of faces around her.

—— chapter 13 ——

Dureena took a moment to gather her wits about her, then slowly got to her feet. The circle moved back slightly to give her room. They looked like a hard-bitten bunch, clad in a great variety of gaudy and ragged clothes. Those present all seemed to be Humans, or of Human stock.

A little back from them, and seated on a raised platform, was an older man, in his mid-forties or fifties, with a tough, wised-up face. It didn't take a lot of insight to realize that this was the leader of whatever she had gotten herself into. And it took no smarts at all to see that her wrists were cuffed in bright steel.

The man on the platform said, "I'm Bishop. I'm in charge of this chapter of the Thieves' Guild. You were having a bad dream. And you have awakened to another. What's your name?"

"Dureena. Dureena Nafeel."

"Do you have the mark?"

Dureena nodded.

"Show us."

Dureena raised her manacled hands. One sleeve fell back to reveal the glyph tattooed on her arm. When one of the women beside him whispered an affirmation to him, Dureena realized that Bishop was blind. An appropriate choice for justice among thieves.

"Who trained you?" Bishop asked. "Who brought you into the Thieves' Guild and taught you our ways?"

"Mafeek, of Tripani 7," Dureena replied.

"Mafeek is known to me. Who was his teacher?"

"Gant the Elder."

"And how long have you been a thief?"

"Long enough to be good at what I do."

Rolf, standing in the circle, smiled unpleasantly at her cockiness. "But not good enough to avoid being seen, captured, and restrained."

Dureena stared him down. "I hardly made a secret of my desire to find you. I wanted to check in as soon as possible, and the best way to do that was to draw your attention. I was captured because I chose to be. But there was no reason to treat me this way. Had I known the level of your hospitality, you would have been the one on the floor, not me."

Rolf said, "You talk pretty good for someone who's chained up."

Dureena looked at him, wide-eyed and mocking.

"What chains?"

As the result of a movement too quick to follow, the chains fell to the floor. Dureena was in full stride before they had landed. Knocking two thieves aside, she grabbed Rolf and, with a single powerful move, threw him halfway across the room.

Rolf scrambled to his feet, his face dark with fury. He was about to come at her when Bishop raised his left hand, freezing everybody in place.

He said to Dureena, "You've made your point. I welcome you, as one Guilder to another."

Dureena relaxed slightly. The all-important first step had been accomplished.

"While you're here," Bishop went on, "you'll follow the rules: Do not interfere with the activities of any other member of the Thieves' Guild, and do not betray our presence to the authorities.

"We support rigged games, pickpocketing, theft, con jobs, black marketeering, and barter, but nothing violent, nothing that would cause the authorities to notice us. We get ten percent of your earnings in exchange for a place to stay and our support. If you are captured by the authorities, you are alone; we cannot help you. Any questions?"

"No," Dureena said.

"Then you can go. I'll have one of the others show you the way."

As Dureena turned to go, Bishop said, "One last thing. You're a long way from home, Dureena Nafeel, wherever that is. I don't think I've ever seen someone quite like you before. What are you doing here?"

Dureena looked at him and shrugged. "I don't know," she said, then turned and left the room without waiting for an escort.

—— chapter 14 ——

Maneuvering the *Excalibur* away from its spacedock was a delicate operation involving carefully calculated forces. The big ship was still inert, not yet under its own power. *Excalibur* was dependent entirely on the tiny tugs that maneuvered it. There were a lot of them, but they came to only a fraction of its mass. An unexpected solar flare or an imprecisely calculated application of power could send the ship crashing back into its spacedock, or spinning out of control into the void. Unlikely, but these things did happen, and heads rolled in consequence.

A master helmsman from the spacedock crew, stationed on *Excalibur*'s bridge, was in charge of the maneuvering. Although it was cool on the bridge, the man was sweating. He was well trained for this, but there was no training that fully prepared one for the unexpected. He was doing the best he could, however, confident that his experience would guide him if the unforeseen arose.

Sheridan came to the bridge during the maneuver. Garibaldi and Drake were there, waiting for him. They all waited breathlessly while the move away from the dry dock was completed. Once that was done, it was less anxious work, towing the *Excalibur* out to the firing range. And when that had been accomplished, the master helmsman saluted the bridge personnel and went to the space lock with his crew, glad to return to the dry dock and be rid of the responsibility. *Excalibur* belonged to Sheridan now, and he was welcome to it.

"Well, we got here in one piece," Garibaldi said to Drake. "That's always a good sign."

Drake looked offended, but didn't reply. Sheridan, who was used to Garibaldi's humor, grinned and checked the power levels as indicated on the control board.

It was time for the weapons test, second in importance only to the propulsion of the ship itself. *Excalibur*'s small working crew—all Rangers, Minbari and Human—were distinctly keyed up, waiting to clear this pivotal hurdle. There was a low hum of expectation on the bridge. Sheridan was aware of the quiet sense of power the ship gave off, even though she was untried, inert, and had passively been towed along by mere tugs. A ship with weapons yet untested, the *Excalibur* still felt like a sleeping giant.

Garibaldi addressed Sheridan now. "Good morning, Mr. President. You're just in time for the weapons demonstration. Shall we?"

"Anytime you're ready," Sheridan replied. "You . . . are ready, I suppose?"

Garibaldi grinned—a dismal sight, given his mood. He slapped Drake on the back, a little harder than was necessary.

"Ready, willing, and able. Isn't that right, Drake?"

Drake moved a little away from Garibaldi and touched his wrist com.

"All hands, prepare for level-one test firing. Repeat, prepare for level-one test firing."

Then, to the crew member who was manning the weapons console, "Weapons control, stand by."

"Weapons control, aye, sir."

With an inquiring look at Sheridan, who nodded, Drake slid into the captain's chair and looked at the monitor. It revealed its target—a small asteroid, white-faced, pockmarked, and bare, turning slowly in space.

He said, "Target twelve degrees by nine degrees by twenty-five degrees."

Control repeated, "Twelve by nine by twenty-five, aye, sir. Confirm target lock."

"Fire," Drake said.

Even with recoilless gunnery, Sheridan could feel the tremor under his feet as the forward guns fired. The first beams of energy shot blue flame as they smashed into the planetoid.

Drake called out, "Cease fire." To Sheridan he said, "What do you think, Mr. President?"

"Well, I'm a little disappointed," Sheridan said. "That's not much more firepower than the average White Star. I thought these ships were going to give a bigger punch."

Garibaldi said, "Then I suppose we'll just have to deliver on our promise. See, that was just level one. Go to level two, Drake."

Drake looked like a man unfairly put upon. "I don't— Sir, we haven't even warmed up the system before today. And there's . . . a complication."

"What kind of complication?" Sheridan asked.

"The enhanced weapons array is based loosely on Vorlon design. They were intended to be used in ships far more advanced then we're capable of building, with a far greater energy reserve. Firing the big guns takes virtually all our power . . . so they should only be used as a last resort."

"Duly noted," Garibaldi said. "Would you care to try out the next target, Mr. President? Say, that big asteroid over there."

Not far from their previous target, a large asteroid, the size of a White Star cruiser, crater-ridden and dead, rolled slowly in the darkness of space.

Drake got out of the captain's chair and went to the acquisition console. Sheridan slid into the captain's seat.

"You may fire when ready," Garibaldi said.

From the console, Drake called out, "Weapons control, level two, ready to fire. Target bearing nine by six by twenty-three."

"Nine by six by twenty-three," control repeated. "Aye, sir. Target locked, ready to fire."

Sheridan glanced up at the target. It had changed. Instead of the blank surface of an asteroid, he was looking at the blue and white face of Earth. He blinked, trying to make the image go away.

"Ready to fire, sir," Drake said, his voice expressionless, his facial expression as good as saying this was a bad idea.

"No," Sheridan said. "We can't . . . How did we—"

"How did we what, sir?" Drake asked.

"That's the Earth out there," Sheridan said.

"What?" Garibaldi said.

"I said that's the—"

Sheridan stopped in midsentence. Looking through the port again, there was no sign of Earth. Only the asteroid's dead face.

"Sir?" Drake said.

"Nothing," Sheridan said. He stared again at the asteroid, his lips tightly compressed. Damn it, was he hallucinating now? Dreams were one thing, but when he was awake, on duty . . . Maybe he *was* getting too old for this.

With an effort, he pulled himself together. "Nothing. Prepare to fire."

"Standing by," control said.

"Fire," Sheridan said.

The lights began to dim. Outside, there was a power buildup at the tips of the *Excalibur*'s left, right, and top structures. There was an audible crackling sound, and suddenly power surged from those points to the front of the ship in a manner reminiscent of Vorlon weapons. The shock was delivered to the asteroid with near instantaneity. The little world was engulfed in a fury of flames. It took less than a second to bring about its complete destruction. Fragments of it formed a confettilike display before the shock wave dispelled them.

On the bridge, the lights continued to dim. Some of the instruments were registering near-failure levels. And a chill was entering the room, as though the heaters had gone down, too.

Although he had warned them that something like this was going to happen, Drake felt strangely apologetic, as if the power loss had been his fault.

"As I said, it drains nearly all of our energy, leaving barely enough for gravity control. We can't navigate or fire again for at least a minute."

"Which leaves the ship vulnerable," Sheridan said.

"Yes, sir," Drake said. "For one minute."

"A lot can happen in a minute," Sheridan said.

When it happened again, Sheridan was ready for it. Or as ready as he could be when the unexpected stepped in and suddenly took control. He thought he was getting used to it, learning to anticipate it, to recognize the warning signs, like the faint thrilling at his fingertips that told him something strange and unprecedented was taking place. It was like a cross between an adrenaline rush and a panic attack. *Crazy or not, I could almost learn to enjoy this,* Sheridan thought to himself. *I hope that doesn't prove that I'm losing it.*

Regardless, the sights around him were growing dim. He knew it was happening again. He could barely make out Garibaldi and Drake.

And then they were gone entirely.

It was strange, but there on the almost-dark bridge, Sheridan could feel first a breeze, then a wind that came up suddenly from out of nowhere and began tearing at him. But that was impossible. You can feel a lot of things in a starship, but wind isn't one of them.

Sheridan turned, trying to figure out where the wind was coming from. He saw at once that he wasn't on the bridge any longer, not on *Excalibur*. He was outside, on a dark plain that extended in front of him as far as he could see. There was a small wood fire burning on the ground nearby. There were six or seven robed figures seated in a circle around it. The figures were silent, mysterious. As his eyes became accustomed to the gloom, he saw that the encampment was ringed by tall stones, reminiscent of Stonehenge.

It had happened again, but this time, it was different. Whatever mysterious power had seized him before had plucked him again from aboard the *Excalibur*. These beings held the answers to his questions, and there was something about them . . . something familiar, despite the alienness of the landscape. No, he wasn't losing it—there was a motive behind his "visions," and he was going to get to the bottom of it.

Glancing upward, Sheridan saw two moons visible in the black velvet sky. This wasn't Daltron 7. The wind rose and fell, and seemed to speak with a voice of its own, then died down as suddenly as it had arisen. The robed figures were talking among themselves, their voices raised in argument.

Despite the robes, Sheridan recognized them instantly. Techno-mages. He had met their kind before, on Babylon 5. Faced with the Shadow menace, the techno-mages had chosen to depart for some unknown region of space. Before they left, Sheridan had been fortunate enough to speak with their leader, Elric.

Elric had left Sheridan with a lasting impression. He had radiated a sense of calm, resolute power. Of knowing his place in the universe. Of knowing when to act, and when to wait.

Despite the agitated nature of their discussion, these robed figures still possessed the indefinable aura that could come only from techno-mages. And they were arguing with one of their number.

One of the techno-mages said, "You shouldn't have brought him here. You're endangering all of us."

Another nodded vehemently. "I agree. It's foolish. Remember, Galen, we agreed to have no contact with outsiders."

So it was Galen again, Sheridan thought. The guy was up to his weird tricks once more.

Galen, standing a little apart from the others, said, "And if our silence means the death of billions? You said I should explain myself to everyone involved. He's involved, whether he knows it or not."

The first techno-mage said, "Galen, this is premature. We can't make contact without proof—"

"But we can't get proof without contacting someone on the outside! This is insanity!"

A second mage said, "Perhaps it is. But these are insane times. And *this* one . . . is he the best you could do?"

"As a matter of fact, yes," Galen said. "He is the one person who can give us what we need."

He paused a moment, then said, "We all know what is at stake here if I'm right. Yes, we must protect ourselves, but in doing so we cannot turn our backs on those we left behind."

"All right," the second mage said. "We will allow this one contact, no more. But if you compromise our hiding place, if we risk death because of your actions . . . understand that you will be the first to die."

And suddenly, in a flash of lightning, all the techno-mages were gone. Only Sheridan remained near the fire, and the tall figure of Galen.

"They're upset with you," Sheridan said.

"Not upset. Afraid. Fear makes wise men foolish. In my case, I can only hope it makes fools wise." Galen stooped and stirred the fire, then looked up at Sheridan. "Do you know who . . . what we are?"

Sheridan said, "You called this an electron incantation. A dead, and probably deliberate, giveaway. You're techno-mages. You use technology to simulate the effect of magic. I met one of your kind before."

He remembered clearly the time that techno-mages had gathered at Babylon 5, on their way to escaping the Shadow War. Sheridan had spoken with one of them, Elric, and he remembered being impressed with the wisdom and character of the man.

His brief contact with these almost legendary characters had had a big effect on Sheridan. He had always regretted that he hadn't had a chance to check out some of the common legends about the techno-mages. It was said that they knew the fourteen words that would make someone fall in love with you, and the seven words to painlessly say good-bye to a dying friend. And that they knew how to rediscover dreams when the world had taken them away.

Galen rose and pushed back his hood so that Sheridan could see him clearly.

He said, "We came to this place during the Shadow War, to prevent our secrets from falling into the wrong hands. Though the war is over, our leaders are in no hurry to return. We will continue hiding for a bit longer: twenty, thirty more years, just to be safe. They like being safe."

"And where are we now?" Sheridan asked.

Another flash of lightning.

"Wrong question," Galen said.

"I'm hip."

"Listen to me carefully, Sheridan. We don't have much time. The connection between us is a delicate one."

Squatting, Galen drew a circle in the dirt. He gestured, and the circle filled with the image of a dark world torn by fire.

"Do you recognize this place?"

Sheridan looked at it, and a bitter memory arose within him. This was where his wife Anna had died. At the hands of creatures whose nightmarish nature still made his blood run cold. "Yes. Z'ha'dum. Homeworld of the Shadows before they left for the rim." And the place where *he* had died.

"An ancient race, dedicated to chaos and destruction. They left, but their allies remained. Some of them you know as the Drakh."

The image in the circle changed to a Drakh face— hideously lined and wrinkled, lips turned down, eyes betraying a bottomless malignancy. It glared out at Sheridan, then, after a moment, disappeared.

Galen said, "We have been watching the Drakh for some time, afraid that sooner or later those who once served other masters would choose to become masters themselves, and continue the work the Shadows began. Lately, we've heard rumors, stories from other races who have encountered the Drakh. We believe they are preparing to move, testing their resources, weapons, and capabilities."

"But with the Shadows gone, their world destroyed . . . how much power can they have?"

"That's what you have to find out."

"Why me?"

"Because I believe they are going to start their war by attacking Earth. Remember, it was Humans who organized the other worlds into opposing their masters during the Shadow War. Such things are not quickly forgotten."

"You said resources," Sheridan said. "How much do they—"

"I've told you all I can," Galen said. "And some of what I suspect. That is all I'm allowed to tell you. The rest you and your companions must learn on your own. But do not tell anyone what you are doing, or why; the Drakh have spies everywhere. If they know we are watching, they will move before we can prepare."

"I don't think anybody'd believe me anyway. The dreams . . . all this . . . they'd think I was crazy. How do I know if any of this is true?"

"You don't," Galen said. "But you're curious enough to want to find out, which is why I chose you. Your spirit is such that you will go, even if it means going alone."

That surprised Sheridan for a moment, made him pause. He knew Galen was right—he would see this through. Did that make him a hero, or did it mean he actually *was* crazy? It didn't matter, really. There was a job to be done.

Galen stared into the fire for a long moment, then said, "I wish I were going with you. I wish I could help . . .

because if what I believe is true, unless you act, Earth will suffer the fate of Daltron 7."

The wind came up again, sudden and lashing, filled with dust and debris. Sheridan thought he saw something in the sky: a familiar object. Then a double-forked flash of lightning split the sky. Sheridan was momentarily blinded. When he could focus again, Galen was gone.

But now there were four circles in the dirt. There was a face in each of them.

One of them was his own. The others were unfamiliar: a savage-looking woman with black hair and wild gold eyes; a man who looked like an African American from Earth; and a being who was unmistakably a Drazi.

He wondered, *Who are these people? What was Galen trying to tell me?* The woman with the gold eyes—he couldn't even identify her race. The African American might be someone in EarthForce, but no one Sheridan had ever met. And the Drazi? What did a Drazi have to do with this?

And while he was musing, something changed. Sheridan looked around. In the sky, replacing the two moons, was the unmistakable outline of Babylon 5.

Then he heard Garibaldi's voice, saying, "Mr. President? Mr. President?"

Back on the now familiar bridge of *Excalibur*, everything seemed just the way he had left it. Garibaldi was looking at him curiously. And Drake was standing off to one side, studying his monitors, ostentatiously taking no notice of Sheridan's lapse.

When he noticed that Sheridan was again paying attention, Drake began speaking.

"I was *saying* that the hull is a plasteel-crystalline alloy, capable of refracting eighty percent of any energy weapon used against it, although that twenty percent can mount up pretty fast in a major battle. We—"

Sheridan stood up abruptly. "We have to go," he announced. *This isn't going to be easy, though,* he thought to himself. If he had doubted his own sanity, he couldn't imagine what the others were going to think. But there wasn't time—the techno-mage had made it clear that the fate of Earth hung in the balance. He'd have to try to explain along the way.

Garibaldi said, "What? But we just—"

"Tell the *White Star* to pick us up. We have to go, and we have to go right now."

"Go where?" Garibaldi asked.

Sheridan thought back to the last thing he had seen when he was with Galen. It had been Babylon 5.

He mused aloud, "It was above the faces . . . over them all . . . Babylon 5."

He left the bridge quickly, without so much as a backward glance.

Garibaldi watched him go. He was becoming filled with alarm. What had happened to the chief? Staring at static-filled StellarCom screens, sleeping at weird hours, blackouts, now this. Was he coming unraveled? What was going on here?

He noticed Drake looking at him.

"You heard the president's orders, Mr. Drake. Call up the *White Star*. We're going to Babylon 5."

He turned away as if this were the most usual order in the world. Drake was an outsider. No sense letting him think his president had gone completely off his rocker, even if he *had*.

―― chapter 15 ――

Sheridan sat, silent, pensive, in the command seat aboard the *White Star*. Around him, one shift of Rangers went off duty, and another came on. Displays danced across the monitors. There was an ever present sensation of power and purpose as the ship knifed noiselessly through space.

Sheridan had some sheets of paper spread out on the console before him. He was sketching the faces he had seen earlier, in the circles in the dirt: the faces that Galen had caused to appear. Although Sheridan had never thought much of his drawing skills, these sketches were taking shape with uncanny accuracy. He wondered if Galen might have stimulated his artistic center. Hard to say what else could account for this suddenly acquired artistry. Perhaps it was simply a response to a command he had received—programming that enabled him to remember these faces, burn them into his memory, find out to whom they belonged.

He was engaged in this drawing when Garibaldi came onto the bridge. Garibaldi's face was a study in itself—the perfect picture of a man trying not to be judgmental. But clearly he needed to know what was going on. He seriously wished Sheridan were being a little more forthcoming. Of course, Garibaldi also knew he often wasn't very forthcoming himself. He couldn't blame John for keeping these matters to himself, whatever they were. But he really needed to find out what was going on.

So he decided to try what he hoped was the casual approach. "So, John . . . Mr. President . . . you want to tell me why we're heading to B5 in such a hurry?"

Sheridan looked up from his drawings, considered for a moment, and said, "No, not yet. Because I'm not even sure I believe it myself. But I have to find out if what I think is . . . *is*."

"I see," Garibaldi said, thinking that this was double-talk if ever he'd heard any. And he'd heard some in his career. Had even put out some.

For the first time, he began to wonder seriously if there weren't something the matter with Sheridan.

"You know, we could stop by Minbar on the way over, just for a day . . . see Delenn," he said, trying to sound sympathetic. "You've been under a lot of pressure lately, and—"

"I'm fine, Michael," Sheridan said flatly. "And we're going to Babylon 5." That was that.

"Right," Garibaldi said. "Absolutely. Whatever you say. I'll just get a little work done while you're . . . drawing."

"Good idea," Sheridan said. "Oh, and while you're at it, see what you can find out about a planet named Daltron 7."

"Never heard of it. Is it important?"

"Could be," Sheridan said, and returned to his drawings.

Garibaldi looked up, saw a Human Ranger at the doorway. He walked over to him and said, "Get me Captain Lochley at B5. I'll be in my quarters."

With a final glance at Sheridan, he left the bridge.

Sheridan didn't even look up. He had almost completed his sketches. He darkened the Drazi's skin, wishing now he had been working in pigments. Still, the face was recognizable. They all were. Now the only question was, who were they, and where?

—— chapter 16 ——

Aboard the Omega-class destroyer *Charon*, Captain Leonard Anderson was commanding. A big African-American man in his early forties, he was standing at the helm. His first officer, Kramer, was hovering nearby, looking more than a little nervous.

Finally Kramer said, "Are you quite sure about this, Captain?"

Anderson turned. "Quite sure, Commander. Why? Is there a problem?"

"No, sir. It's just . . . our last message from Earth-Dome ordered us to the Vega Colony for a routine security patrol. And now we've changed course to Babylon 5 without notifying HQ."

"Phil, you worry too much. Now go on with the status checks. I know what I'm doing."

The first officer nodded dubiously. "There's also an officer from the engine room, sir. Flagler. Looks like he's got a grievance. Shall I deal with it?"

"No. I'll take care of it myself. Send him to me in the wardroom in ten minutes."

* * *

Flagler entered and saluted smartly. He was a small, skinny man with a head of unruly red hair and thin, unpleasant features. They usually indicated trouble. Anderson had dealt with him before. And he had a good idea what it was about this time.

"Another complaint, Flagler?"

"Well . . . Yes, sir."

"What is it this time?"

"Well, sir, I'm speaking here largely on behalf of the crew."

"That's understood," Anderson said, the irony in his voice barely noticeable.

"We—they—were all promised leave on Vega. That's what we were told, sir, official-like."

"That may be true," Anderson said. "But the duties of the ship take precedence over leave. You know that. You were told that right at the start."

"I do know it, sir. But the stuff I was told said that good and sufficient reasons would always override planned rest periods."

"Yes, and so?"

"So, begging your pardon for being so bold, sir, there seems no good and sufficient reason for this trip to Babylon 5. And what it means, sir, it means some of the boys will miss some important appointments." These appointments, Anderson knew, consisted of an all-Vegan poker contest that started in two standard days.

"It'll help you save some money, Flagler. I remember you didn't do so well the last time we got to Vega. Got skinned, if I remember correctly."

"Yes, sir, that's true. But it's still my God-given right

to throw away my money if I've a mind to. And we need our R & R."

"True enough, Flagler, and I wish I could accommodate you in this. Unfortunately, we need to go to Babylon 5."

"Yes, sir, so you say, sir. But I was looking at the ship's schedule—it's posted, sir, I wasn't trying to sneak anything—well, sir, that posting says we go to Vega."

"That's where we *were* going. And now we're going somewhere else."

"Yes, sir. But by whose orders?"

Anderson stiffened. His normally cheerful face became harsh with anger. "Are you questioning my orders, Flagler?"

"No, sir! That is, not exactly. But those orders of yours were never countermanded, sir. Sparks received no orders to the contrary. A fair-minded man, sir, might think you were taking us to B5 on a whim of your own, or maybe on some personal business."

"Be careful what you say, Flagler. You could get yourself into a lot of trouble with this line of talk."

"I don't want to do that, sir. But at the same time, we have our rights, all of us, officers and enlisted. We got a right to our leave on Vega. Maybe you got a right to go to B5 to pursue whatever interests you. No one's denying that. But the Vega run is important to us, and if it's just a case of your whim against ours—well, sir, a good officer will listen to a complaint like that. No offense intended, sir, but it's not right to whip us halfway across space just because you want to visit with somebody."

"That's quite enough," Anderson snapped. "I'm not

going to explain my actions to you. I'll just tell you that this move of mine is far from a whim. I have reason to think that EarthForce security is involved. That's reason enough for this trip."

"Yes, sir. But EarthForce doesn't seem to feel that way. That is, they never authorized your change of plans. They're going to be very surprised when they find out."

"That's between me and them," Anderson said.

"Yes, sir. You and them and the inspector general."

"Are you threatening me, Flagler?"

"I wouldn't dream of it, sir! But there are set routines for differences of opinion between officers and commander. I mean, you aren't Captain Bligh and this isn't the Royal British Navy."

"Right. And you're a long shot from being Fletcher Christian. That will be all, Mr. Flagler. Unless you care to pursue it further. But I warn you, you do so at your peril."

"No, sir, I haven't anything more to say. I just wanted you to know that there are appropriate measures for this sort of thing, and I intend to follow them."

Flagler stared at Anderson defiantly.

"That will be all," Anderson said, and he watched, stone-faced, as Flagler saluted and left the wardroom.

—— chapter 17 ——

Leonard Anderson. A skilled player of the five-string banjo. Phi Beta Kappa at the University of Kentucky at Lexington. With a doctorate in astrophysics from Dartmouth. A colonel in EarthForce, commanding and piloting *Charon*, a first-class destroyer.

Leonard Anderson, sitting back in the command chair in a dimmed room, found himself thinking back on the long way he'd come to achieve all this.

Where he'd grown up, a few of the old electric trains had still been operating. His father had been a conductor on the Delaware-Lackawanna railroad, running between Hoboken in New Jersey and Central Station, Philadelphia.

Back then, when he was little, Anderson had sometimes ridden with his father. He had loved the old cushioned seats in the passenger cars, and the way his father had reversed their backs at the end of a run, setting them up for passengers going the other way, back to Lackawanna station in Hoboken. When they left Brick Church station, Leonard would always watch for the big Sherwin-Williams sign, which stood on a hilltop near the tracks, just before they entered the tunnel.

It was a neon sign, and it showed a big globe with white and blue lines of longitude and latitude. A neon boy in a Dutch sailor's cap stood above the globe, holding a can of paint. There was an illusion of motion as the boy tilted the paint can. Red paint spilled out and engulfed the globe. It became a crimson sphere, slightly larger than the sun, which, in Leonard's memory, was also setting nearby.

When he was very small, that neon globe had seemed to him a real planet. And the Dutch boy had been a giant of some sort, sinister in spite of his blond hair and sunny smile. The Dutch boy was killing the planet with his can of deadly paint. That was how young Leonard saw it.

In grade school Leonard had learned of the planet Venus. It was slightly smaller than the Earth, so his teacher had said. Leonard had wondered if it might not be Venus that the boy was covering. And, he surmised, the red paint must be making it hot, because he had learned in school that Venus was too hot to support life. But when he asked, his teacher had assured him his neon planet wasn't Venus.

Leonard forgot his questions about the Sherwin-Williams globe after a while, but he continued to think about Venus, became fixed on the idea of going there in his father's train. When he learned that wasn't going to be possible, he decided he'd have to find another way.

Though it wouldn't take him to another planet, he still rode the train: a thing of power, snorting steam; the slow and then more rapid rise and fall of the pistons; the heavy panting noise of the engine as it turned the massive driveshafts; the slow movement of the steel wheels, the train beginning to come to life, a waking giant, and then moving faster, with irresistible force.

He came to love that feeling of power, and he wondered if it was anything like the sensation astronauts experienced as they hurtled toward the stars. Wondering turned to desire, and that steered him toward his most coveted goal—a spaceship command.

But the road that would take him there wouldn't be an easy one.

His parents were killed in a car crash when he was fourteen. Leonard had been at a school-sponsored camp in the Catskills. He had no near relatives, and was too proud to ask help from distant kin, so he dropped out of school and went it alone in New York City. There he learned the bitter truth: that no matter how good people said the economy was, for some, there were no jobs.

He couldn't get work without a work record. He couldn't get a work record without working. So he did a lot of hanging out. He might have gone the way of a lot of kids. You saw them hanging out in the inner cities. Hustling, stealing, robbing stores, but mostly just hanging out. Waiting. Waiting for nothing.

But then he got his first lucky break—a job as a roustabout and beast of labor on the old *City of Birmingham*, one of the first spaceships on the Earth-Io-Europa run. All that was required was ceaseless and unremitting slave labor.

Back in those days, the roustabout was needed to do all the physical stuff, because the various skilled-labor unions didn't permit their pilots, navigators, or even their cooks to so much as lift a garbage can if that wasn't called for in their job descriptions.

That was all very well for the union members, but who was to do the grunt work, all the lifting and heaving, the carrying of wastes to the disposal unit, the endless stowing and restowing of the cargo? All the chores it didn't pay to automate.

That was Anderson's work, and one of the unwritten but very real requirements for the job was that the holder of the job be grateful for the opportunity to kill himself with overwork in only a couple of years.

Anderson didn't like the attitudes of the people for whom he labored, but he forced himself to do what was necessary, and even to do it with enthusiasm. He earned a lifetime of experience in that job, learning to motivate himself. He lived through it, and his sheer dogged determination proved instrumental in enabling him to move up the ladder, to become a steward.

In this new position he served a lot of pilots who thought they were hotshots. He served their stuffed-shirt friends. And he waited on politicians.

William Jeshke, a senator from Kentucky, was touring Io and Europa on some sort of junket. Leonard couldn't see any valid reason for the senator to be spending so many taxpayer dollars; to him it seemed like a colossal waste.

But Jeshke must have seen something he liked in the young man, because he enjoyed expounding his views to Anderson late into the evenings, over a bottle of Kentucky corn whiskey.

Anderson stayed away from booze, figuring he had enough working against him already. And listening to Jeshke, Anderson became even more cynical. Men like Jeshke made ideals sound cheap, reduced them to tools that they used to ingratiate themselves with a gullible public.

"Son, I wish I could pour you a drink," Jeshke said one such evening, lounging on his cot in the little stateroom that had been assigned to him aboard the *City of Birmingham*. "But booze is allowed only to passengers, not crew. Sorry about that."

Anderson shrugged, and looked at the man curiously. Jeshke was a big, florid man with beautiful white hair and benevolent features. His face and his general bearing, calm and dignified, had gotten him into office. They had gotten him this freebie trip. They *hadn't* earned him Anderson's respect, however. The young steward had developed a built-in aversion to this kind of smooth operator. He knew enough to keep his opinions to himself, but his skill at dissembling hadn't been enough to keep Jeshke from noting the undercurrent and calling him on it.

"You don't like me, do you, son? I understand you're in no position to talk about it, but I hereby grant you permission to say whatever's on your mind. You will not be the loser for it."

"I have nothing on my mind, sir," Anderson replied, remaining stoic all the while.

"Son, I can also understand your being cautious; a man in your position has to be. But when you've been expressly asked to say what you think, and you refuse to do so—I don't mean to be harsh, but that smacks to me of cowardice."

"I've got a lot to lose," Anderson noted candidly. "That's a pretty good reason not to speak out."

"Pure coward mentality, loud and clear, son," Jeshke baited.

Anderson's hands balled into fists. "Are you calling me a slave?"

"No, I'm saying you've got a coward mentality," Jeshke replied without wavering. "It's a very different thing."

Anderson took a step forward. He looked dangerous at that moment. Though young, he was large, with a musculature that had been well-developed by endless hours of manual labor.

"I hope you ain't thinking of striking me, son. That's a liberty I don't permit. But I'm still interested in your opinion of me."

Anderson hadn't really been planning to attack the man. He had taken the step toward Jeshke in the heat of the moment. As that anger had passed, he found it replaced by . . . curiosity.

"Why do you want to know what I think of you?"

"First you answer my question, then we'll get to yours. And sit down, you look tense standing there."

"You seem to think you know a lot about me."

"You're a lot like I was at your age. You think you have the whole world pegged. But you don't, really. For example, what do you think you can tell me about people like me?"

"You're hypocrites," Anderson said. He had made up his mind and was rushing his words now, so they wouldn't trip in his throat. "People like you talk about patriotism, but you're really just looking out for number one. You claim to be serving the people, but you take handouts for trips other people can't afford. A lot your state of Kentucky cares about what goes on on Io or Europa!"

"You got a lot of assumptions running there, son," Jeshke said. "What makes you think any of them are true?"

"Stands to reason," Anderson said. "Everyone knows—"

Jeshke held up a hand and interrupted him. "Saying 'everyone knows' is the same as saying no one knows. Or don't you think so?"

Anderson wanted to argue, but he was too bright, and too honest with himself, not to realize that his generalization about Jeshke would be just as unreliable as any generalization Jeshke might make about him.

"So why *did* you come out here?" Anderson asked instead.

"To learn something and to do something."

"What do you think you'll learn?"

"I have to learn what it's like out here. And I have to do this for the sake of my constituents. The people of Kentucky may not build many spaceships or even train any pilots, but they're just as much a part of the Human race as anyone else, and if the future of mankind is out in the stars, they need to know about it, too."

"I don't see why."

"You don't have to build spaceships to have a stake in where they go and what they do once they get there."

"But you already know all that! The television and the papers are always going on about space."

"They still haven't come up with a substitute for a man finding out for himself, and going back to report on what he found to his neighbors."

Anderson discovered he had no answer for that one. After a while he said, "And what is it you're going to do?"

"That will remain my business until I've done it. Unlike many politicians, I believe I know when to remain silent. Good night, son, and thanks for stopping by. It's been nice talking to you . . . Leonard Anderson?" He read the name badge on Anderson's lapel. "I won't forget that."

Anderson never spoke to Jeshke again. Throughout the run to Europa, Anderson kept expecting something to happen to him. As they landed he even wondered if Jeshke might have him arrested on some trumped-up charge. After all, Jeshke had made a point of noting his name. That had to mean something.

But nothing happened. Not then. Not until eight months later, when the *City of Birmingham* returned to Spaceport Newark on Earth.

Soon after the ship docked, the purser gave Anderson a message. He was to report to the local military commander, whose office was located in the old castle above the heights of Fort Newark. The purser claimed he had no idea what it was about, but he indicated Anderson had better move along. And while he was at it, he might as well take along his gear.

Anderson reported as ordered, certain he was in for it now. And he was, but not as he'd imagined.

The port commander revealed that Congressman Jeshke had established a scholarship for him. If he accepted, Anderson was to report at once to the space cadet training center at Dartmouth in New Hampshire.

It was like a dream and a prophecy come true. Service

in EarthForce involved travel to distant worlds, worlds that all too often needed someone to save them from destruction. In those cases, someone was standing in for the diabolical Dutch boy—sometimes aliens, sometimes Humans.

Thinking about it now, he realized that the planet in need of saving was Earth. The diabolical Dutch boy had become a Drakh—and the red paint enveloping the Earth was almost certainly a legacy of death left behind by the Shadows.

That much had been revealed in his dreams, by the strange, hooded being who had contacted him. The being who called himself Galen. The being on whose word he was proceeding—against orders—to Babylon 5 and a situation he couldn't yet truly imagine.

—— chapter 18 ——

Ni'im the Drazi was on the second day of his visit to the small planet that circled Hennesey's Star. He was carrying a load of rewired miniature motors to sell to the small colony there.

The colonists were a dull-eyed, apathetic bunch and suspicious of strangers. They hated buying from Ni'im on general principles. But they needed his small motors for their many farming projects. Ni'im did a good business.

He was really tired, and he needed a good night's sleep. Getting to Hennesey's Planet had been no piece of cake. It had been a slow, difficult, tedious job, navigating through the dense asteroid belt that surrounded Hennesey's Star and its single planet. He got a good price for the motors. But it all made him very tired.

Ni'im went to sleep in his rented quarters and woke up on a desolate plain, with fires burning across the broken landscape. He knew at once it was a dream, but he wasn't surprised by it. He'd been having a lot of weird and upsetting dreams of late. He was ready for this one.

"Look at it, Ni'im," Galen said, gesturing toward the ruined land. "And ponder its meaning."

"Who are you?"

"I am Galen."

"I know the meaning of this dream," Ni'im said, a note of defiance in his voice.

"And that is?"

"You're warning me to do what you tell me—or I'll wind up in a place like this."

"That's an odd sort of reaction," Galen said.

"I've been waiting to tell it to your face."

"But I've never met you before," Galen noted.

"Not directly, no. But you're the one who's been sending me the nightmares. And now you think you've softened me up so you can make me do what you want."

Galen was genuinely surprised. This was not at all what he had expected. It hadn't gone this way with the others.

Galen said, "I don't think I'm getting through to you."

"You're getting through just fine," Ni'im said. "That's a cute trick, transporting me here. This *is* a dream, isn't it? I suppose you've manipulated my astral body. Is that how it's done?"

"Something like that," Galen answered.

"It'll do you no good. I'm on to your tricks."

"My tricks? Who do you think I am?"

"You're one of them."

"One of who?"

"The enemy."

"What enemy are you referring to?"

"The Drakh, that's who. The only real enemy."

"This is preposterous," Galen said. "Look at me. Do I look like a Drakh?"

"Of course not. What would be the point of that?"

"I'm afraid I don't follow."

"A Drakh trying to get me to do something would of course disguise himself. For whatever reason, you've chosen to appear as an Earther. Though frankly, you haven't done a very good job of it."

"Where have I gone wrong?" Galen asked.

"The features. No Earther ever looked like you look."

"First I ever heard of it. I don't look like a Drakh, though, do I?"

"You look like someone trying to disguise himself in a dream as an Earther. But essence will out. I know what Earthers look like, and you're not one of them. Lucky you didn't try to disguise yourself as Drazi. You'd really have botched that!"

"This is crazy," Galen said. "What could the Drakh possibly want from you?"

"That's what I'd like to know," Ni'im said.

Galen looked disgusted. "I'll get back to you later."

"Take your time," Ni'im said. "You won't get anything out of me."

Galen broke off the contact and sat very still for a while, frowning. He was alone in his darkened room, sitting cross-legged on the floor, illuminated by the light of a single powerglobe. He was disturbed.

His plan called for contacting four people. That was the minimum number he needed to make it work. He had selected them with care, had found just the ones he needed. His order had been aware of Sheridan ever since Galen's teacher, Elric, had encountered him years earlier. His will made him a perfect choice.

Success seemed to be within his reach. His only problems had seemed to lie entirely with his fellow techno-mages, their reluctances, their timidity.

He hadn't counted on difficulties among the four he needed to contact. Initial skepticism, yes. Downright refusal, no.

But he should have known that visions of the sort he dealt in inspired different reactions in different people. And the reactions of non-Humans could be more problematic still. Something to do with their internal wiring, perhaps.

The Humans hadn't been too difficult to manipulate.

Ni'im the Drazi was something else.

Ni'im was suspicious even for a Drazi. Paranoid might be a better word for it.

Galen realized that he should have picked someone else. But now there was no time. Ni'im was essential to his plan. But how to get him to cooperate?

—— chapter 19 ——

The *White Star* came out of the jumpgate and took up position near Babylon 5. Standing by was Captain Elizabeth Lochley, the officer in charge of Babylon 5. She was dark-haired and serious-looking, with dark, piercing eyes. Her no-nonsense appearance could not hide the fact, however, that she was a beautiful woman, though she seemed more than a little uncomfortable with that.

She had come to Bay 17 in response to the message from the *White Star*, announcing the arrival of President Sheridan and Mr. Garibaldi. They were requesting an urgent meeting.

She paced up and down, wondering what this was going to be about. Lochley admired Sheridan. Hell, they'd even been married, though only briefly and a long time ago. Just out of officer's school. Still, there had been something about him that had made her do it, and that "something" still existed today. He must have felt the same—he had been instrumental in her getting this posting. She knew that she owed him. But this job was her baby, and she wasn't going to allow anyone, not even Sheridan, to interfere in the way she ran the station. Thus, it seemed at times as if she took pains to be critical of Sheridan, as though it was the only way she could keep her judgment toward him sound.

And it seemed to her that trouble followed Sheridan wherever he went. This was doubly true of Garibaldi, so she had a shrewd idea that trouble was going to land on her as soon as they set foot on B5.

The lock door slid open with a smooth purr of oiled machinery, and Sheridan stepped out, followed by Garibaldi. Lochley noticed that Garibaldi already had on his don't-ask-me expression. This piqued her interest even more.

Sheridan said, "Captain . . . good to see you again."

"And you, Mr. President," Lochley responded. "It's quite a surprise."

Sheridan nodded, then with a glance at Garibaldi, said, "Well, perhaps not *that* much of a surprise. I need a favor, Captain. I want you to run these pictures, see if you can find them on the station. The likeness may not be exact, but they should be close enough for the computer to do an analysis."

Lochley accepted the drawings and looked through them. "Are you sure they're here?" she asked.

"No," Sheridan said. "But if they're not, they will be soon. Unless, of course, they've already left."

Sheridan then walked on into the station, thus indicating that the time for discussion had ended. Garibaldi and Lochley exchanged meaningful looks.

Lochley said, "Do you have any idea what this is about?"

"Not a clue," Garibaldi answered with a touch of exasperation.

They followed Sheridan into the station.

* * *

Dureena was in the Zocalo. It was a crowded place that seemed filled to overflowing with people and things. It was Babylon 5's marketplace, a place where you could find anything and sell anything. The proclivities of a dozen or more different races, evenly divided at present between Human and other, vied for attention here. The fantastic variety of clothing alone would have served to outfit the cast of a futuristic presentation of *The Beggar's Opera*.

The Zocalo gave the impression of having been compressed to fit the confined, curving surfaces of Babylon 5. It was an entirely indoors landscape, a riot of colors, many of them faded to earth shades of brown and gray, as though returning to their remote origins. Here and there was a patch of orange, a rust patch that had erupted overnight in the moist atmosphere and escaped the cleanup people and the refinishers.

Dureena loved it here. She enjoyed the sounds of this small, densely crowded city within a city, especially the sounds of people, talking, wheedling, arguing, laughing, shouting—the great symphony of denizens packed closely together and trying to live by the customs of a former life that involved more space.

The effect was an analogue of a medieval scene, from a time before people and things had become standardized. And the wares of this marketplace were every bit as exotic as the buyers and sellers, ranging from book decoders that projected eyelid images to basket lunches that could be eaten in odd corners, wherever the diners could perch.

And as rich as the shifting shapes and images were,

the extraordinary array of sounds competed with them for attention. The variety of speech-noises, ranging from squeaks to droning basses, mixed with an overlay of sounds generated by the station itself: metallic noises produced as parts worked against each other, internal sounds like the flow and gurgle of the various pipes carrying liquids, the lapping chuff and hollow boom of other tubes filled with gases of various sorts.

Dureena glided through the Zocalo as if it were her natural element, even though she had never seen a place as crowded, congested, and various as this. She was munching a granidos, a molded protein substance flavored and deep-fried and sold by vendors. Dureena thought it was the most delicious thing she'd ever eaten. She had quite forgotten the subis with baked draff bread of her home planet. This stuff was better!

Vlast was behind her once again, keeping his distance, practicing his art of blending in with whatever crowd he was passing through. An unobtrusive fellow was Hycher Vlast, small, hunched, furtive, and easy to overlook. His ragged black clothing matched the apparel of half the Humans here, and more than a few of the aliens. He moved with his head down, but cast quick looks through bright eyes that lurked behind a tangle of coarse black hair. But strangely, despite his best efforts, between one glimpse and the next, he lost sight of the woman.

"Damn it!" he said to himself. How could she have eluded him so easily? What secrets had she learned on whatever far-flung planet she'd been raised on?

"Looking for me?" a voice said in his ear.

Vlast whirled. There was Dureena, standing less than

a yard from him, her look most unpleasant, even alarming to behold. Vlast noticed that she had a jagged piece of metal in her hand, its end taped.

"I thought they took away your weapons at customs," Vlast said.

"There's plenty of stuff lying around here—if you know how to use it."

"Hey, not on me, lady!" Vlast said. "I mean you no harm."

"Then why have you been following me?"

"You noticed that, did you?"

"A blind man would notice your interest in me, little man. And I'm not blind."

"No, that you're definitely not," Vlast said. "Believe me, lady, I mean you no harm. Quite the contrary. I knew you were the right one the moment I laid eyes on you. I'm here to offer you the opportunity of a lifetime."

"Serving you, no doubt? Forget it. I'd rather mate with a slime mold."

"I meant no such thing," Vlast said indignantly. "You're not my type, anyway. No, what I had in mind was to make you rich beyond your wildest dreams."

"This out of the goodness of your heart, no doubt."

"You and I would share equally in the good fortune, depending upon the successful conclusion of a fortuitous combination of your skills and my knowledge."

Dureena scoffed at him, disgusted by his doubletalk. "You're obviously a beggar and a cheat, and the only thing you know how to do is make up tall tales in order to cheat the innocent."

"You, innocent?" Vlast responded. "Lady, I'd judge

you a walking weapon, and a master thief to boot. Oh, don't look so surprised. I had you spotted as one of the Guild from your first entry into Babylon 5. And I was sure of it when Rolf coldcocked you, then took you to Bishop."

"Were you there?" Dureena asked.

"No. I didn't see that part. But I heard about it. I stay well away from Guild meetings. It doesn't pay to pry into thieves' secrets. But that's what Rolf always does when there's a new arrival who shows thieving tendencies but suffers from a lack of credentials."

"I have my credentials," Dureena said.

"That much is obvious, now. Otherwise you would never have walked away from the Guild meeting. As good as Bishop is at thieving, they say he's even better at hiding the bodies of those who don't meet his criteria."

"You know a lot about the Thieves' Guild."

"I've had my dealings with them before. Bishop and I were friends once, and Rolf used to dine at my table, when I had the wherewithal to set one."

"And now?"

"We had an unfortunate falling-out. Pity, because I have an interesting project for which I need a good thief. It is something that could enrich the thief and myself."

"So you said earlier. Why didn't you make a deal with Bishop when you were still friends?"

"Before I take someone into my confidence, I have to feel certain I can trust them. Our disagreement came before I felt I could show these to Bishop *or* Rolf." Vlast's hand snaked into his layered garment and came out with a half a dozen photographs. He handed them to Dureena, who glanced at them with minor interest. They were old, ragged around the edges, and blurred.

"Big deal," Dureena murmured. "Judging from the level of skill shown here, I'm betting you took them yourself." She handed them back to him.

"I beg of you, study them. They will confirm the story I'm about to tell. In fact, they will tell you the story better than I can."

"This is growing tedious," Dureena said. "Am I supposed to do this standing here on this street corner?"

"Permit me to buy you a drink," Vlast said smoothly. "We are no great distance from the Red Hawk Bar. I run a modest tab there."

"I could use a drink or two," Dureena said. "And some dinner, too."

"This way," Vlast said. "And you need fear no foul play in the Red Hawk."

"Glad you told me that." Dureena was sarcastic. "Really makes me feel a lot better. Lead the way."

—— *chapter 20* ——

The Red Hawk, nestled in Down Below, proved to be a Quonset-shaped building wedged in between a curving wall and a stacked pile of thick concrete pipes no one had found a use for yet. The atmosphere was dark, streaked with layers of grime left by the smoke. There were flashes from concealed lighting that did little to help you find your way between the tables.

Vlast passed something to the bouncer, a huge Human in a black T-shirt, and they were ushered to a booth at the end of the room. No sooner were they settled than a waiter came by, a Llort, Dureena guessed, to give them a menu that was printed on heavy cardboard. Vlast ordered for them both, suggested a local beer, and didn't even frown when Dureena agreed but asked for a shot of whiskey on the side.

When the drinks had been served, he handed Dureena the photographs again. "The tale is brief," he said, "and it will tell you who I am and what I am doing here. It will also give you a very broad clue as to what I desire of your skills."

Dureena sipped her whiskey, drank down half the

107

beer, and scanned the photos, this time affording them more attention.

One photo portrayed a stately room on a planet that—through a large picture window—boasted a yellow atmosphere streaked with violet. In the room stood a gaudily dressed man with a crown—seemingly the ruler of the place. And there was another man whom she had no difficulty in recognizing as Vlast—but a younger Vlast, and much better dressed. In fact, a Vlast who actually seemed a person of consequence. The other pictures showed different views of the same scene.

"Okay," Dureena said. "I've seen them. So what?"

Vlast said, "These were taken at a court ceremony on the planet Myost. You don't know of it? No reason you should. You don't look to me like a lady who has studied celestial geography. Pickpocketing 101 is perhaps more your speed, eh, my lady?

"Myost was a small world, and it was in the path of the Shadows during the Great War. I was minister of finance in the government of the planet. Securing the planet's treasure was my line's hereditary task."

Vlast took a long drink of his beer, then resumed his tale.

"In view of the menace, I recommended the evacuation of our Homeworld. It was already obvious that the Shadows would overrun us as they had done so many others. Our treasure, I told the king, should be used to buy us passage to some safe haven.

"The king ignored my advice. He placed his trust in treaties, secret treaties with many fine clauses. Finally I was able to prevail upon him to let me take our national treasure off-planet, to hide it on Babylon 5. Then, if anything went wrong, the treasures of our culture, at least, would not be lost."

Vlast took a final drink of his beer. "And now it is over. My people are gone. My planet is a dead world. Nothing remains of Myost but me and the treasure. That treasure is now on this station."

"So what do you need me for?"

"I need help to reclaim what is rightfully mine."

"Yours? I thought it belonged to your people."

"So it did. I am the last survivor."

"Then why can't you just walk in and take it?"

"The storage company has, shall we say, arranged matters to make this all but impossible."

"The storage company?"

"Their contract provides for a period of time after which, if the treasure is not removed, the company can claim the contents for itself. Therefore, they have good reason to make entry into their lockers as difficult and dangerous as possible. They alone reap the benefits of red tape and vague contracts."

Dureena thought about it. "Your tale of how the treasure got here has more than one inconsistency."

"Perhaps," he replied. Then his eyes narrowed. "What do you care what the truth of the matter may be? Perhaps I stole the treasure and brought it to Babylon 5 myself, only to have it stolen from me. Or perhaps someone else did take it, and I killed him. What difference does it make? There's a treasure here, and I'm offering to share it with you."

Dureena looked at him thoughtfully. Vlast might be a liar, but he might really know where something valuable was to be found. What did it matter to her how it had gotten there or to whom it really belonged?

So she said, "Is *any* of that story true?"

"Enough of it," Vlast said.

"I'm going to be very annoyed if the treasure isn't where you say it is."

"And I," Vlast said, "am going to be equally annoyed if you're not up to the task of acquiring it for me. It's here on Babylon 5, that much is the truth, and it's not going to wait for us forever."

—— *chapter 21* ——

Vlast led the way, about ten feet ahead of her, his black clothing flapping in the wind sent up by one of the ventilators. They were out of the main corridors now, moving quickly through some sort of structure that appeared to be composed of joined boxlike members.

Suddenly Vlast came to a stop in front of an opening, approximately three yards across and five high, in the far end of the structure.

"What's the matter?" Dureena asked, glancing around for signs of trouble.

"The next bit is a little tricky," Vlast said. "I'd appreciate it if you'd go first."

Dureena studied the opening, vaguely visible in front of her by virtue of a faint glowlamp in the ceiling. She didn't much like the look of it. And there was a faint odor, one which she couldn't quite place . . .

"Isn't there a back way we can use?"

"This *is* the back way. It's the only way we can get to the lockers without setting off the alarms."

That set off faint alarm bells ringing in Dureena's mind, but she moved ahead, her senses on the alert. She moved through the square doorway. Even as she did so, she identified the strangely familiar odor—ailgii! She spun around to turn back, but a panel slid into place behind her, covering the opening before she could get to it. She heard another metallic clang and a hatch slid shut nearby. Automatic lights came on and she saw that she was trapped inside a square box about three yards to a side. Furiously she kicked at the door. It didn't give.

She realized now that she was in a compactor box, of the sort used to press masses of ailgii, an edible fungus grown commercially on Alcestis 2. She had recognized the characteristic odor an instant before the trap had sprung, but too late to do anything about it. Ailgii gave off a sweetish grassy sort of smell, with a faint peppery tang to it. Unmistakable, once you had grown accustomed to it.

"What in hell is this?" she shouted. "You've trapped me!"

"Not at all, Dureena." Vlast's voice came to her faintly from the outside. "I've done a great deal of research. This is the only way of getting to the storage lockers without setting off the alarms."

"Through the ailgii-compacting vat?"

"It brought *me* to a stop," Vlast admitted. "But a lady of your talents should have no trouble dealing with it. It's about time I learned how good you are at getting out of tight places."

"Let me out of here," Dureena said, her voice piercing and dangerous.

"Get yourself out," Vlast said. "Then I'll know for sure about your talents. And the way ahead will be open for us."

"When I get out," Dureena said, "I'm going to kill you, Vlast. Slowly. Painfully."

"You'll change your mind when I show you the treasure," Vlast said. "It's big. Oh, it's very big, Dureena. I'm going to take you there. All you have to do is oblige both of us by getting out of the compactor box."

Dureena had a few other things to say, but decided to use her time more usefully. She looked around, more carefully this time.

She was in a sealed metal box. That much was apparent at a glance. The floor beneath her feet was dusty. The recessed fluorescents glowed dimly, providing a faint light without shadow. At the box's midlevel there were inspection ports, one to each side, with windows that were reinforced with heavy metal mesh. Through the window on one side she could see Vlast. The meshed port on the other side afforded a view of a passage that, in turn, led through an archway lit by a glowbulb. It led, presumably, to the lockers where the treasure was stored.

The compactor was empty, offered nothing she might use to break the Plexiglas. That was immovable, obviously welded into place. Looking around, she saw that the ceiling was slightly different from the rest of the box. It was a solid square of bright metal that fit inside the walls of the box, with a fit too tight to put a knife blade into.

Nonetheless, Dureena pulled a knife blade out of her pocket, one of several plasteel weapons she had concealed when giving Zack Allan what had supposedly been all her armament. Its heft helped her to concentrate.

She moved to the wire-mesh opening in the front of

the box and looked out. She was able to see a circuit box on the wall. The box had two big buttons, one red, one green.

There was a hum of machinery, then a heavy metallic scraping sound. Glancing up, Dureena saw that the ceiling of the box had begun to inch down toward her.

"Did you do something?" she called out to Vlast.

"Nothing! I believe the compactor box turns on automatically whenever anything is introduced into it. I've heard that the specifications call for a crushing force of one and two thousand pounds to the square inch. This obstruction stopped me, but I have no doubt you have some trick up your sleeve."

Dureena again glanced up at the ceiling. It was descending very slowly, but with an awful finality. The scrape of metal on metal made a nerve-shattering screeching sound. It must have gone a long time between lube jobs.

Without hurry, Dureena reached into her clothing. She took out a flexible piece of cord that might have been mistaken for a part of her garment. She bit off a piece of it and crimped the cord twice with a peculiar motion. She placed it on the narrow ledge where the Plexiglas was inset, then stepped to the back of the box and turned away.

There was a brief, sharp explosion. Shards of Plexiglas, too small to hurt her, flew everywhere. Dureena turned back to the mangled mesh and pushed it out. It dropped to the deck with a tinkle.

From his position behind the compactor box, standing on tiptoe and peering into the inspection port, Vlast figured out what she had done. "Very nice," he said.

"But perhaps you didn't notice that the opening is too small for a lady of your goddesslike proportions."

"I wasn't planning to crawl out through it," Dureena said. "Though I could manage if I had to. No, I just wanted to clear some space for this."

She reached into her hair and pulled out something. It was crescent shaped, and Vlast thought it might be some kind of a hair clip or ornament. He changed his mind when, with an economical but powerful sidearm motion, Dureena threw it through the front port she had just opened.

The missile struck the red button squarely and solidly. The machinery turned off. The ceiling stopped descending. There was a click of circuits, and the front and back of the box opened.

Vlast stared, scarcely believing what he had seen.

"You can step through now," Dureena said. "It isn't going to bite you, and neither am I—for the moment. Now can we get a look at this treasure?"

—— chapter 22 ——

Moving more quickly than before, they went through more corridors and connecting passageways, past more ancient debris and clutter.

"Doesn't anyone ever clean up this place?" Dureena asked.

Vlast shrugged. "I've never been here before. As I told you, I never got past the compactor box. The ailgii processing system hasn't been used since the time of the Shadow Wars. The rest has been set aside for valuables sent to Babylon 5 from planets trying to survive the Shadows. Each planet was assigned its own automated locker space, and allowed to make whatever provisions were considered necessary to preserve its goods.

"But in the desperate rush that prevailed at that time, no one really checked the credentials and backgrounds of the companies who claimed to be storage providers. Unscrupulous operators preyed on the desperate races who were fleeing the Shadows. The storage company brought the goods to Babylon 5, but they no doubt changed the codes so they would have easy access, should the treasure owners be killed."

The passageway narrowed again. The light became murky, and as they went through a tight turn, they found themselves in darkness. The glowlamps had been extinguished in this part of the station, or had burned out.

Pulling a small, handheld lamp from a pouch, Dureena led the way, moving forward slowly, cautiously, watching each step.

Almost immediately she felt that something was wrong. She could sense something waiting in the darkness, some presence darker than the absolute blackness that hovered outside the narrow beam.

"What's going on?" Vlast asked. "What's the matter?"

"Be very still," Dureena said. For at the sound of his voice she had heard something stir in the darkness, felt the slight movement of the air as something moved.

"But I—"

"Shut up!" she hissed.

She listened, every sense straining. She had picked up the faint, almost subliminal hum of machinery.

She smelled the dusty air and the faint trace of machine oil. With infinite care, she took a step to the left, then another, and another after that, bringing her to the corridor wall. She moved slowly: it would be disastrous now to blunder into any movable object. She could tell that the thing, whatever it was, was moving again, but more slowly. She could hear the almost imperceptible noises it made as it quested, turning this way and that. Always avoiding the flashlight beam.

Then she heard Vlast, a few feet away from her, his

voice quivering with fear, whispering, "Dureena? What can you see?"

She didn't answer. But the thing in the darkness gave a single creak at the sound of Vlast's voice. It had come to a stop about six yards to her right, as far as she could tell.

Dureena willed Vlast to speak again, and he didn't disappoint her. She heard his hoarse whisper.

"Dureena—what is it?"

On the basis of almost imperceptible subcues, she could sense the thing as it tensed, heard it as it coiled, preparing itself for a leap . . .

She timed it perfectly. Kicking out with every ounce of energy in her body, she caught the thing in midair, just as it launched itself at Vlast.

Vlast squealed involuntarily and tumbled backward, crying, "Help! It's got me!"

Dureena had no time to attend to Vlast. She dropped the flashlight—things were happening too fast for it to be of any use. She followed up her kick with a stride and then a plunge into the darkness where she knew the thing was. She could hear it scrabbling around on its back, making audible clicking sounds now as it tried to right itself. And then she was on it.

It was smaller than she had imagined, perhaps the size of a large cat. Her hand closed on its head. She wrenched, releasing and focusing her energy with a shout that echoed throughout the corridor. The creature's metallic head came off in her hand. The thing quivered, its limbs twitched, and it expired.

Vlast scooped up the flashlight. After he'd recovered enough to realize he was not injured, he managed, with shaking hands, to turn it on their assailant. They examined the creature that had been stalking them. It was a small, spiderlike metal thing. Smoke arose from its interior circuits.

"I've heard of these things," Vlast said. "It's a vermin catcher. A lot of storage facilities use them nowadays. It's battery-operated, with motion sensors to detect rats or anything else that scurries around in the darkness. They're supposed to be programmed not to attack something as large as a person."

"The owners of this storage facility wanted to keep out vermin of any size," Dureena commented. Throwing the mechanical remains off to one side, she continued, "Shall we get on with it?"

Another short walk brought them to an anteroom lit by ceiling glowbulbs. It seemed to have been a receiving dock of some sort. There were benches, and an unmanned desk with a dusty communicator and a keyboard. Behind the desk, a closed metal door apparently led to the storage area itself.

"At last!" Vlast breathed. "I can't tell you how long I've waited for this moment. Imagine it, Dureena! The lockers must lie just behind that door. And the treasure of Myost awaits us."

"First we have to get through the door," Dureena pointed out.

"I don't suppose it just pushes open," Vlast said, giving the door a shove. It was immovable. "I was afraid not."

He studied the door. "No handle or locking device. No visible hinges. Nothing but a single big steel plate. Damnation! Could we have come this far for nothing?"

"Obviously," Dureena said, "the door isn't meant to be operated manually."

"How, then?"

"Whoever comes here must communicate with it by the computer." She studied it. Though it was covered with dust, its ready light was on. She tapped a key. A program came up on the screen. It read, "Entry level. Authorized personnel only. Password required."

"This may not be too difficult," Dureena said. She sat down in front of the computer, rested her fingers on the keyboard, thought for a moment, then typed, "Password."

There was a hum of small servos kicking into life, and the metal door slid smoothly open.

"How did you know that?" Vlast asked.

Dureena shrugged. "I figured it was no big secret, just a matter of form. This used to be a manned station. People came in and out of here every day. Whoever ran this facility didn't want to simply leave the door open. But there was no reason to make getting through it difficult, either. Anyhow, all of the traffic would have to have been service facility personnel. If anyone else had gotten this far, they must have already proven they were authorized."

"Then why a door at all?" Vlast asked.

"How should I know? People put up doors whether they need them or not. Maybe they wanted to avoid drafts. Shall we go in?"

Inside was another, larger room. It was the storage facility. There were lockers on all the walls, from floor to ceiling, square containers about two yards to a side.

They had markings identifying their planet of origin. Myost's locker had a double-crossed arrow symbol marking its place of origin.

Dureena studied the setup. She saw that entry into the locker was controlled by a keypad.

"See if you can open it," Dureena said.

Vlast punched in a series of numbers. The locker didn't open.

"The operators of this facility must have changed the codes," Vlast said. "Make it easier for them to get at the goods when no claimant turned up. No wonder they didn't have to lock the door. You can't get into your locker anyhow!"

"We should be able to find the correct code, anyhow. It probably isn't buried very deeply."

"Maybe not. But who are you going to ask?"

"The computer, of course."

She went back to the desk, Vlast following. Sitting down, she called up a menu of programs. Since the computer was dedicated to the single task of control-ling the storage facility, this wasn't difficult. She found a help file and called up a screenful of definitions.

"Here's what we want," Dureena said. "Access codes." She typed in the words. The computer re-sponded by requesting the locker number.

"What are the coordinates of the Myost locker?" she asked Vlast.

Vlast told her, and Dureena keyed them in. Immedi-ately, a series of numbers came up on the screen, listing all of the units in that area of the facility. She moved the cursor to the appropriate locker, then hit "unlock."

"That should do it," she said.

They went to the locker. "So let's open it," Vlast said.

"Be my guest," Dureena said, stepping back.

Vlast went up to the door, again dialed in the access code, and turned the handle. It turned easily. Dureena took another few steps back, watching him carefully.

Even so, the power of the resulting explosion took her by surprise. She was aware of being propelled through space, coming up hard against something, then everything went black.

When she returned to consciousness, she found she was lying on the corridor floor. Bishop was standing over her.

"Where in hell did you come from?" she asked.

"I heard you were hanging out with Vlast, so I assigned someone to follow you. You're new here. You couldn't be expected to know the man's reputation."

"I figured him out for myself," Dureena said, carefully getting to her feet. She was bruised and sore, but there was nothing broken. "What hit me? Never mind, I know. Vlast is dead, isn't he?"

Bishop nodded. "How did you figure?" he asked.

"I had a suspicion it was getting too easy. Having the code right there, easy to access. There was no way of telling, but I thought there might have been some sort of final booby trap. Vlast found it the hard way. Better him than me."

"If you figured out that much, how come you got caught in the blast?"

"I didn't figure anyone would use three times the amount of explosive needed," Dureena said ruefully.

"Well, live and learn. Thanks for looking in on me, Bishop. I'm okay now."

Bishop smiled. "I also thought you might need a little help getting the loot out of here."

"Maybe I would," Dureena said cautiously.

"Unfortunately, there's nothing there. The locker's empty."

"Damn! Where could it have gone?" Dureena said, pounding her fist against the wall. "Judging by what Vlast said, that was a lot of treasure!"

"Maybe the guys who set up this scam figured there was too much valuable stuff to leave lying around," Bishop commented, and Dureena noticed he avoided looking her straight in the eyes as he continued. "They could have put it into another of these lockers, or shipped it to any of a dozen other worlds. I don't suppose we'll ever know." Suspicion began to blossom, but she didn't dare challenge him—clearly he was too powerful. So she shrugged.

"Well, it was an interesting adventure, though unprofitable. Tell you what, I'll buy you a drink later, Bishop. You did look out for me—after checking on the loot."

"Fine by me," Bishop said.

But as it turned out, Babylon 5 security had different ideas for Dureena.

—— *chapter 23* ——

Early in her career, Dureena had come across an aging thief—a rarity, since there really wasn't a great life expectancy in her trade. He had told her the secret of his longevity. "There are a lot of distracting things out there." He had made a vague gesture to take in the entire universe. "Don't let yourself get distracted. More people are brought down by distraction than by bad plans."

Dureena had found that to be good advice. For the most part, she had followed it. It was too bad, she thought, mulling it over afterward, that she hadn't followed it this time.

She was going through the Zocalo . . .

And then she noticed the man. He was a tall, skinny Earther, dressed in a faded red velvet suit. He had a long neck and a prominent Adam's apple. She noticed that he had big feet, and they were encased in high-top, lace-up shoes of the kind only rural types wore.

He looked like he'd just stepped off the space launch, just arrived at Babylon 5. He had that raw, earnest look about him, the look of a man amazed by what he was seeing and trying hard not to show how much he was impressed by it. He looked like a small-time carny worker. And he was setting up a game right in the middle of a corridor.

She came closer and studied his features. On closer scrutiny, she decided he had two looks: one part of him was a naive country kid, and the other part was a wised-up country kid. She wasn't sure which look was true. It might be interesting to find out.

He carried a folding table under his arm. He set it up, and from one pocket he took three silver thimbles. From an inside vest pocket he extracted a little golden pea, which he held up to show to the few people who had stopped to take a look. He turned it in his fingers, catching streaks of light from the overhead glowbulbs.

He said, "It's a pea, my friends, just an ordinary pea, but it's made of gold. Not solid gold all the way through, but twenty-four-carat gold-plated. It's worth something, friends, maybe a hundred credits. I'll put this object of intrinsic and artistic value up against your money. Fifty credits secures the bet. But I've got cash, too. I'll wager any amount against an equal amount. I'll bet you can't find which thimble the pea is under. The hand is quicker than the eye, friends. Or is it? Watch where the pea goes."

Dureena knew at once what he was up to. This was a version of an old Earth game called three-card monte. In the playing-card version, you tried to find one card— an ace, perhaps—while the handler moved it and two queens back and forth. In the cup version, you tried to determine which cup or thimble the object was hiding under. Either way, the sucker lost.

Although a lot of people knew the game, there were

always some who didn't. Or some who thought they could outsmart the sharper. Professionally interested now, Dureena watched as he manipulated the thimbles.

The first thing she noticed was that he wasn't very good. His motions were slow, clumsy, and a fine tremor shook his fingers. Dureena decided this guy wasn't going to be in business long. Not only were his motions clumsy, he was manipulating the golden pea in such a way that it made a faint clinking sound as it came into contact with the side of first one thimble, then another. It was very faint: Dureena wasn't sure she could find the pea by the sound alone. But there was someone else in the crowd who had caught on to this and was stepping forward confidently.

It was an Emyr from Ogden 6. This race, of remote lemurian ancestry, was characterized by large pointed ears that could swivel 180 degrees and tilt up or down through 12 degrees of arc.

"You seem pretty sure of yourself, young man," the lemurian said when the kid had finished his manipulations. "Might I look at your hands?"

The kid held them out. The lemurian grabbed them both, immobilizing them.

"Hey! What's the idea!"

"I just want to make sure you stop here. I'll take your bet, young man."

"Let's see your money," the kid said.

The lemurian nodded toward the crowd. "May I have some assistance?"

A large shaven-headed man in a black leather vest came up and took over holding the rube's hands.

The lemurian reached into his wallet, took out fifty credits, put them down on the table.

"You still confident?" the lemurian asked.

"I am!" the rube said.

"You really got any money?"

"I got plenty! Leggo my hands!"

The lemurian nodded at the shaven-headed man. He released the rube, who took out a billfold stuffed with credits.

"This enough for you?" he asked.

"I'll take another fifty," the lemurian said. "Anybody else want to get in on this?"

"Hey, just a minute," the rube said, as he seemed to notice the lemurian's ears for the first time.

"You said you'd wager whatever we put up," the lemurian reminded him. "Everyone here will hold you to that promise."

There was a murmur of agreement.

"Anyone else want to get in on this?" the lemurian asked.

Others in the crowd had heard the click of the pea against the side of the thimble. And enough knew the hearing skills of lemurians. Half a dozen came forward and put down their own wagers. There must have been a thousand credits on the table before they were through. The man in the vest counted out a similar amount from the rube's billfold, then handed it back to him.

"I think we're ready now," the lemurian said cockily. "But one of *us* will pick up the thimble. Not you."

The rube looked as though he wanted to complain, but the crowd growled at him and he agreed, with a poor grace.

"Now, friends," the lemurian said, "I personally heard the pea hit the side of the thimble on the left. But does anyone else have a better idea?"

Several in the crowd muttered, but decided to leave it to him.

"Then here we go," the lemurian said. "Here is your pea!" He lifted the thimble.

There was nothing under it.

"Damnation!" the lemurian cried. "He must have palmed it!"

He lifted the next thimble, and then the one at the far end. Under that one lay the golden pea.

Dureena had anticipated something like this. She watched as the rube picked up his winnings and moved away quickly. The lemurian was busy explaining how it must have happened. "He must have clicked the thimble with his fingernail. It sounded just like the pea striking it. Damn it, I'm out fifty credits!"

He strolled off, muttering under his breath.

Dureena thought the lemurian's explanation had some merit to it. But more than likely, the rube and the lemurian were partners in this short-time grift.

Not that she was about to reveal that to the suckers.

They got what they deserved.

A moment later, a Hyach buyer caught her attention. He was leaning over a display of miniature etchings inscribed on synthetic jewels. His purse, dangling from his belt by a string, looked nice and enticing. It would be fun playing with the money, she decided. So she moved past him and, with a single deft move, cut the purse and tucked it away. He didn't notice a thing . . .

But someone else did.

Two someone elses.

Zack and his men had been scanning the Zocalo all morning, looking for the people depicted in President Sheridan's drawing. They had received copies, along with a demand that they observe the utmost confidentiality in this matter.

None of the three had shown up yet on Babylon 5, not even the Drazi, who was ugly even by Drazi standards and hence easily recognizable. But no one had seen him. The security officers had begun to think this was a wild-goose chase, until they spotted the woman. There was no mistaking her; Sheridan's drawing had caught something of her savagery and independent attitude.

The officers exchanged hurried glances.

"Let's get her!" one of them said.

With a single accord, they jumped into the crowd and tackled Dureena before she even knew they were there.

Once they had her, however, it took another two station personnel to help them keep her down. Zack notified Lochley, who showed up almost immediately. She gave Dureena a long, searching look. "Well, I'll give you this one," she said. "She's a dead match for the drawing."

—— chapter 24 ——

In the station commander's office, Sheridan and Lochley were looking at a screen that displayed Dureena's picture and the drawing side by side. There was no doubt about it. The two were a match.

"Who is she?" Sheridan asked.

"You don't know?" Lochley responded. "But you drew her."

"It's a long story. What's her name?"

Lochley consulted her notes. "Dureena Nafeel. She arrived a few days ago. Judging from the half dozen purses and wallets she was carrying when the guards got her, I'd say she was a petty thief."

"But a good one," Sheridan said. "To steal that much without anyone noticing . . . Where's she from? I've never seen an alien like that before."

Lochley checked a file on her desk. "Zander Prime." She frowned. "But . . . I thought that was a dead world."

"It is," Sheridan said. "Now. Zander Prime was wiped out during the Shadow War. During the last days of the war, the Shadows revealed one of their biggest weapons . . ."

As he spoke, the image formed up in his mind. Once again he saw the deathcloud reaching with tentacles of darkness toward a planet . . . The cloud was a thing almost too huge to conceive.

"It was capable of engulfing whole worlds," Sheridan went on, seeing it happen again, seeing the cloud, inky black and still expanding to fill all the visible horizon. And then the missiles began to pour in, thousands of them, a silvery rain of missiles.

"Thermonuclear missiles from the deathcloud penetrated deep into the planetary core, where they exploded, destroying the planet from the inside out."

His mind filled for an instant with the explosion of a world, splitting into a thousand fragments, molten magma pouring out from its core, its surface stripping away in the titanic blast like shredded skin stripped from a burn victim, mountains tumbling into space, oceans vaporizing.

He shuddered slightly despite himself. "Zander Prime was one of the last planets destroyed by the Shadows. We thought no one had survived. Until now."

Lochley said, "I told her we were going to throw her off the station for theft. We'll bring her by to see you on her way to deportation. Might make her a little more cooperative."

Just then, Lochley's link *breep*ed. She toggled it. "Yes?"

It was Lieutenant David Corwin, her second in command. In a flat voice that still betrayed his excitement, he said, "We've got a Captain Anderson on the line. He wants to speak with the president. Says it's urgent."

"All right," Lochley said. "Put him through." Then she asked Sheridan, "You know this guy?"

"I don't think so," Sheridan said.

Anderson's face—a dark, square, handsome face with a quiet dignity to it—appeared on the monitor.

Anderson said, "Hello, Mr. President. By any chance, have you been looking for me?"

Sheridan and Lochley looked from him to one of the two remaining drawings. It was another match.

"So it would appear," Sheridan said.

Half an hour later, Sheridan and Anderson were shaking hands in the conference room on Babylon 5.

"Mr. President," Anderson said.

"Captain. So you were drawn here, same as I was."

"Yes, sir," he answered. "It's good to meet somebody who won't think I'm crazy if I say 'the man in my dreams told me to find you.' "

"If you're crazy," Sheridan said, "then we're both crazy."

Just then the door opened and Dureena walked in, somewhat warily, but defiantly nonetheless.

Sheridan turned to her with a smile. "Ah, good. Dureena Nafeel, this is Captain Anderson. I'm President John Sheridan, and we—"

No sooner were the words out of his mouth than Dureena dived for him with a wild yell. They both went down in a tumble of limbs. Anderson and the guards quickly jumped into the fray, helping peel her off Sheridan, who got to his feet.

"Let go! I said let go!" Anderson said to Dureena,

who was still struggling, even as Sheridan got to his feet. "What's the hell's the matter with you?"

Dureena shouted at Sheridan, "My world is dead! My people, my family, they're all dead . . . And it's your fault!"

— chapter 25 —

When you're running one of the ten biggest corporations on Mars, you have a lot of paperwork with which to contend.

Michael Garibaldi didn't like paperwork.

Lochley had given him an office on Babylon 5, and Garibaldi had papers strewn everywhere. Although he had only been using it briefly, the place was already a mess. There were papers in transparent folders stacked on the filing cabinet, and papers in colored cardboard folders covering his desk. There were stacks of memos marked URGENT—ANSWER IMMEDIATELY. There was a list of messages, all to be answered yesterday. There were more papers stacked on the floor. These were the slightly less urgent ones.

Garibaldi sat at a desk in the middle of it all, tapping a pencil against his teeth, seething. Usually he found it exhilarating, running Edgars Industries. He had taken over the position following William Edgars' death. At about the same time, he had married Edgars' widow, Lise, who had been Garibaldi's own true love before the booze and misunderstandings had driven them apart.

He and Lise had a daughter now. Mary was six months old, and she was the light in Garibaldi's eyes. And he had this pharmaceuticals company, to use not just for profit but as Edgars had used it, to further projects he considered important. *Unlike* Edgars, Garibaldi was partial to projects that yielded benefits to mankind.

Edgars had been funding a lot of black projects, shady investments that were often more trouble than the daily cutthroat operation of the company. They required a great deal of ongoing attention, as did many aspects of cleaning up the mess in which Edgars' untimely death had left the company.

In spite of this, Garibaldi enjoyed what he was doing. Right now, however, his attention was scattered.

He got up and paced up and down the office. He looked at the papers again. No, he just couldn't concentrate. There was something on his mind and he just had to get rid of it.

He buzzed an assistant on the intercom. "Where's Lochley?"

"She's in her office. I believe she's very busy right about now."

"No problem," Garibaldi said.

He strode purposefully out of his office, past the startled aide, and down the corridor. He came to Lochley's office door. There was a guard outside, who started to say, "The captain is busy right now—"

"She's about to become busier," Garibaldi said, as he pushed past the man and went on in.

Sitting behind her desk, Lochley looked mildly startled when Garibaldi burst in. Then she realized who it was, and surprise was replaced by irritation.

"Don't you ever announce yourself?"

"Not when I'm in a hurry," he answered, barely registering her retort. "Look, I got something on my mind, and I gotta say it."

She eyed him levelly. Arguing, of course, would be futile. "If you gotta say it, you gotta say it. Would you like a coffee?"

"I'm wired enough as it is."

"Then what's bothering you?"

"Sheridan. Do you think he's losing it?"

"I don't know," Lochley said, serious now. "I mean, on the one hand, two of the pictures he gave us panned out. On the other hand, it could be random chance. The only thing I do know is that he's not behaving rationally. It's almost as if he's acting under some kind of outside influence."

"Could be," Garibaldi said. "All this started after he got a signal that was supposedly from Delenn. The signal was a mess. I figured it got scrambled en route, but it *could* have been a coded message, downloaded directly into his brain somehow."

"Well, there don't seem to be a lot of choices," Lochley said. "Either something really is happening, or someone is making him believe it is, in order to . . . what? Discredit him and the Alliance?"

"Maybe," Garibaldi said. "All we can do for now is keep an eye on him. If he's right, we need to be there to help him. If he's wrong, we may have to intervene before someone gets hurt." He turned and left as abruptly as he had arrived.

An idea had occurred to him, one he didn't feel he could share, not even with Lochley. He knew somebody he could talk to about this—someone who might be able to make some sense out of it all.

—— chapter 26 ——

Shortly thereafter, Garibaldi seated himself in Dr. Irwin Meyer's study in Babylon 5's infirmary and tried to look as if he weren't worried.

He hated sick bays, hospitals, dentists' waiting rooms, and everything else connected with disease and dysfunction. He distrusted doctors on general principle, and he *really* distrusted psychologists, psychiatrists, psychoanalysts, psychotherapists, and anyone in the shrink profession, no matter what name they went by.

His distrust of psychologists stemmed in part from his drinking years, when they had always had something to say that made a man feel small, that had made him feel as though he had given in to some great weakness.

The fact that he was here to consult one of those people didn't make him happy, but what else was there for him to do? The matter had gotten serious, and he was in need of an expert opinion, or what passed for one on Babylon 5.

A student nurse opened the door and looked in. "Dr. Meyer will be with you in just a moment."

"Swell," Garibaldi said, hating her bright, perky

face. He looked at his fingernails and glowered at them. Right now, not even his fignernails looked normal. Somehow they appeared—neurotic.

The door opened again and a large, balding, round-faced man with a bristling salt-and-pepper mustache came in. Dr. Meyer was wearing a white coat, and his necktie was pulled loose. He gave an appearance of slightly vague erudition. Garibaldi hated him on sight.

"Mr. Garibaldi! Sorry to keep you waiting. Just had an appointment to clear up."

"Nothing serious, I hope," Garibaldi said politely.

"Just paranoid delusions. Run-of-the-mill sort of thing around here. I gave him a shot of triparafane and told him to get a good night's sleep. Now then, what can I do for you, Mr. Garibaldi?"

"For me? Nothing," Garibaldi said. "I'm fine, just fine. I came to see you about someone else."

"And who might that be?"

"I'd rather not say."

"I see," Dr. Meyer said, making a notation on a little pad. "And could this person in question not come himself?"

"He isn't aware that he has a problem," Garibaldi said. "In fact, I'm not completely sure he has one, either. That's what I want to talk to you about."

"I see," Meyer said, and he hummed under his breath as he made another note. "Might this person under discussion be an employee of yours?"

"He might," Garibaldi said. "And he might not."

"Might he be someone in a position superior to you?"

"That's also a possibility."

"Hmm." By this time he was writing furiously. "You don't give me a lot to go on."

Meyer continued writing until he found that he couldn't move his fountain pen. That was because one of Garibaldi's hands had closed gently but firmly over it. Meyer looked up, startled.

Garibaldi said, in a gentle, carefully modulated voice, "Dr. Meyer, when you asked Edgars Industries to sponsor your application to Babylon 5 so you could conduct psychological studies here, did you happen to notice the signature of the person who approved you?"

Meyer blinked. "No. I can't say that I did."

"It was mine," Garibaldi said.

Meyer blinked again. "That was very good of you. These studies of people in space, under unusual forms of stress, are of great importance to the body of psychological knowledge."

"And even more important to the career of a certain Dr. Irwin Meyer," Garibaldi said. "Or am I wrong about that, Doc?"

"No," Meyer said slowly, reading the tension in Garibaldi's voice and reacting to it cautiously. "These studies, no matter what their result, will serve to enhance my professional standing. But there's nothing wrong in that, is there?"

"Nothing at all," Garibaldi said. "So we *could* say that it would do you no particular good if your study was prematurely terminated, like, by the middle of next week, and you were sent back home with your tail between your legs. Psychologically speaking, of course."

This time Meyer just stared at him.

"But of course," Garibaldi said, "for all I know, it wouldn't mean anything to you."

"I would prefer to stay," Meyer said slowly. "I would very much prefer to stay. Mr. Garibaldi, if I have offended you in some way—"

"Now we're getting down to it," Garibaldi said. "No, Dr. Meyer, you haven't offended me. Not yet. And I hope that, as our little conversation continues, you will continue to not offend me with a bunch of stupid questions that have nothing to do with what I've come here to find out from you."

Meyer might have been a touch pompous, but he was not stupid. He said, "Let's start over again. How may I help you, Mr. Garibaldi?"

"That's more like it," Garibaldi responded, almost cheerfully. "I'm here to get your opinion on someone I know. Someone whose sanity I have reason to question. This someone's name, rank, and serial number must remain strictly confidential, and will not be revealed, even to you. Just hear what I have to say and let me have your best guess. Okay?"

"Perfectly satisfactory," Meyer said. "Hypothetical surmises are not outside the province of the psychological sciences."

"I'm sure glad to hear that," Garibaldi said. "That takes a load off my mind.

"This individual I'm talking about has been having a series of weird dreams. He doesn't want to talk about them, but at least he's let me know he's having them. Doctor, there's no need for you to write this down."

"Oh, sorry," Meyer said, quickly capping his fountain pen. "Dreams, eh? Psychology still has a way to go to be able to claim a complete understanding of dreams—"

"No kiddin'," Garibaldi said. "Okay, look, this guy can dream whatever he wants, as far as I'm concerned. Dreams are a man's own business, right? But what bothers me is when this guy starts making decisions based on those dreams."

Meyer nodded. "In the ancient world, dreams were frequently considered portents, and acted on—"

"I'm talking about here and now," Garibaldi interrupted. "So kindly save the historical survey for your students. This officer—I guess it's okay if you know it's an officer—has recently made a decision affecting—Christ, you've got me talking like you—this officer has recently sent an expensive piece of machinery on an unauthorized and incomprehensible mission involving a lot of people to a place he had no intention of visiting before he had the dream. He's using up valuable time having people search for other people he's seen only in his dreams. He has a real sense of urgency about all this, acts like the sky will fall down if everything he says isn't acted on faster than quickly.

"What I'm worried about is, he's apt to make more decisions based on data he alone knows, because it came to him in dreams. That's the situation, or as much of it as I can reveal to you at present. Hell, that's all I know."

"I see," Meyer said. "And your question?"

Garibaldi stared at Meyer for a long time. Meyer fidgeted, uncomfortable under that baleful gaze.

After a while, Garibaldi said, "You know, it can be good to talk to someone about your problems sometimes. I didn't know what my question even was until you asked me. I thought I was going to ask you something completely different. Now I know what I really want to ask."

"And that is?"

"Do you think there's some chance that this man, whose hunches have so often proven correct in the past, might be on to something, despite the craziness of his behavior?"

"Hmm," Meyer said.

"You can say that again," Garibaldi responded, getting to his feet. "The question is, 'What do *you* think, Mr. Garibaldi?' And my answer to that is, 'I think that, in terms of his record and his years of service to the great causes of mankind, this guy ought to be given a chance to prove himself.'"

"That's your considered opinion, is it, Mr. Garibaldi?"

"It is, and thanks a lot, Doc, for making it clear to me."

Garibaldi stood up, shook the doctor's hand. "Needless to say, this conversation is not to be repeated to anyone, and certainly not to be written down in any form, not even in your diary—if you keep one. Understood?"

"Understood," Meyer said.

"Then I'll be on my way," Garibaldi said, "and thanks again. Maybe you psychological types aren't as weird as people say. You've got a lot of common sense, despite your somewhat unfortunate manners."

Meyer sat at his desk for several minutes after Garibaldi left. At last he said, to no one in particular, "And you military types have more psychology than I for one would have credited."

Then he got up and went back to his scientific studies, having given enough advice to the perplexed for one day.

── *chapter 27* ──

Dureena was seated now, and quiet, though it had required two guards to tie her arms to the chair. Sheridan pulled over a chair and sat down in front of her as the guards left. The only other person in the room, Anderson, remained standing.

"I don't understand," Sheridan said to her. "Why did you say I killed your world? There was a war, and both sides—"

"We had nothing to do with this war of yours," Dureena said angrily. "We were neutral. When other worlds near us were destroyed by the Shadows, we called to you for help. You did nothing."

"There was nothing we *could* do," Sheridan said. "Our forces were spread out all over the place. Other worlds were being threatened. We were barely holding on. We didn't even get word about your planet until it was too late. By the time we got there—"

"You could have done something!" Dureena said.

"No," Sheridan said. "For years after the war, I asked myself the same question: Could I have done more? Could we have saved more lives than we did? But the truth is, even if we had heard about it in time, we didn't have anything that could stop a Shadow Planet Killer. We were outgunned."

He peered earnestly into her face, then said, "Dureena, you're angry with me because you see me as the symbol for what happened in your world. But I'm not responsible. The Shadows gave the orders. But they weren't the ones who pulled the trigger."

"What are you talking about?" Dureena asked.

"The Shadows had others working for them, who carried out the orders. They're called Drakh . . . and the Drakh are still out there, Dureena."

Dureena hesitated, this new data at war with old convictions. She saw Sheridan again as she had seen him in her dream. But this time his image shimmered and was replaced by a Drakh.

The conflict in her was evident. She seemed scarcely to notice when Sheridan untied her arms.

"You're looking for a target," Sheridan said, "a way to make someone pay for the death of your world. You picked me because you thought you couldn't get to them. But you can. I can give you a chance to strike back at the people responsible for the death of your world . . . before they do the same to someone else."

Dureena rubbed her wrists. Sheridan could almost see a new resolve growing in her. She said, "Then perhaps that is what the dream meant. I thought they were memories of what was . . . But perhaps they were warnings about what is yet to come."

While she was thinking about this, Anderson began studying the drawings Sheridan had made, now spread out on the table.

"Mr. President . . . one thing. There are three of us in these drawings. Where's the other one?"

"The Drazi?" Sheridan said. "I don't know . . . And that worries me."

"Should we wait for him to get here?"

"No," Sheridan said firmly. "If Galen was right, and the Drakh are preparing to move, any delay could cost us dearly. We have to go, and hope he catches up with us later."

Dureena had stood up and moved to the table. She was holding one of the drawings Sheridan had made.

"It's true," she said. "This *is* me. But I don't understand. Why us?"

"I don't know," Sheridan answered. "All I can assume is that we each bring something unique to the mission that will increase the odds of success."

"Speaking of which," Anderson said, "we've got a problem. The forces you're talking about are beyond anything I've fought before. My ship can take us into the fight, but against odds like this, you're going to need something a lot bigger and nastier than an Earth destroyer."

Hearing this, Sheridan's face lit up with an idea. He said, "I think I may have just the thing."

—— *chapter 28* ——

Ni'im was feeling very depressed, and he was filled with self-doubt. This was unusual for a Drazi. Normally, members of his race remained rather simplistically enthusiastic, if rather single-minded.

He gazed out a dirty window and saw the low, gray-brown hills of Alquemar Point, the last place in the galaxy a being with any sense would want to be. The trading had gone well, as usual, but Ni'im had had little taste for it. The haggling over the consignment of machine tools had been tedious, interminable.

Now he stretched out on the bed in the squalid little boardinghouse he was using as his temporary headquarters on Alquemar. At last, he thought, he could get his first decent sleep in a long time, and then he'd be on his way.

He slept.

And dreamed.

He found himself in a gigantic cavern, a gloomy place with stone pillars rising to the low ceiling. In the distance he could see a light, a blue-white glow that seemed to beckon to him. He walked toward it, picking his way with care over the pebble-strewn, uneven ground. He was sure he had never been here before, but he also thought he knew the place well, or had known it once, or would know it someday.

As he moved toward the light, he saw, ahead of him, a circle of figures standing around a low stone altar. They were Drazis, but he had never seen them before, though at the same time he thought in some fashion he *did* know them. There were twelve of them; the youngest was old, and the oldest looked ancient beyond measure. They were chanting something in words he couldn't make out. But they stopped when Ni'im approached.

In his normal waking mode, and even in his sleep, Ni'im would have reacted to this with suspicion. But for some reason, while it was actually happening, this all seemed very natural to him, in the way that many dreams, no matter how bizarre, seem perfectly natural as they run their course.

"I really don't know what I'm doing here," Ni'im told them. "I hope I'm not interrupting anything."

"Not at all," the oldest said. "We were waiting for you, and passing the time by singing a hymn to the beauty of life in twelve-part harmony."

This, too, was very strange, but not unprecedented. In the extensive folklore of the Drazi, there were stories of ancestors who appeared and offered good advice to their descendants.

"Please continue singing," Ni'im said.

"There's no time for that now," the old Drazi replied. "We're here to advise you."

"And what do you advise?"

"That you continue on the path of the dream you have received."

"But why?"

"Because this is a matter of racial survival. We are your ancestors. Twelve of us have been chosen to manifest at this time, but there are countless others. The Drazi race extends deep into the past."

Ni'im had never heard this before, but strangely caught up in the spirit of the dream, he accepted it without comment or hesitation.

"I'm flattered," he said.

"This is a matter involving the future of your own race. It will be dangerous for you. But we, your progenitors, care nothing about individual danger. Each and every Drazi will die eventually. From our point of view, all that is of importance is the survival of the race."

"You're saying the Drazi race might die out if I don't follow the dictates of the dream?"

"Precisely. But this is your choice. Choose well, Ni'im. Control your impetuous nature and you should come out of this safely, and acquit yourself with honor."

The figures started to waver and turn transparent. Ni'im cried, "Wait! I've many things I want to ask you! There are matters you haven't explained—"

"You have all the necessary information," the elder said. "The rest is up to you.

"Farewell."

The figures faded out.

After a moment, the cavern faded out.

And Ni'im awoke in his room on Alquemar, more than a little perplexed. Had he really dreamed of his ancestors?

And, of course, his earlier question, as to whether dreams could lie, still remained unanswered.

The thought occurred to him that maybe the dream hadn't come from his ancestors at all. Maybe somebody had faked it, pretending to be his ancestors.

Maybe Galen sent it. Maybe it was all part of a scheme to confuse Ni'im, turn him into a traitor.

And maybe it wasn't.

There was no certainty. He was just going to have to make a choice—and hope for the best.

He could only wait for Galen to return. Ancestors or not, he needed to check this one out.

Meanwhile he had work to do and more stops to make.

—— chapter 29 ——

The arachnids of Chloris 5 weren't on anyone's list for intelligent species of the year. Maybe that was because it took three of them to carry on a conversation about the weather, and at least five to conduct a simple business transaction.

Still, once they got it together and got coordinated, they could haggle away with the best of them.

That, at least, had been Ni'im's experience. The Drazi had been buying silk from the arachnids for several years. He always came away satisfied with the result, but he always had to watch his step. The arachnids were old hands at fobbing off second-rate goods in place of the good stuff.

Five Chlorisian arachnids were lined up in front of him in the mouth of their cave, their hairy arms waving this way and that. Four of them were talking at the same time, arachnid style, with a lot of high-pitched squealing. The fifth was producing silk, spilling it out of his mouth by way of his special glands.

Number one was saying, "Look at the texture! The color! The sheen!"

Two was saying, "O, the tensile strength, so remarkable."

Three was saying, "Unique! And priceless!"

And four was saying, "A steal at four credits an erst!"

It was the usual sales pitch. Every line, repeated endlessly, until the buyer gave in, often out of sheer frustration, or the sellers got hungry and lowered the price.

Ni'im had already evaluated the arachnid's production. This batch wasn't really very good. Maybe he was suffering from tired glands. Ni'im could still make a profit on the stuff, but not at four credits an erst.

The arachnids yammered in their shrill voices. Ni'im shook his head and made the arachnid sign of refusal—an L shape drawn in the air with an emphatic hand—and he wondered, not for the first time, what he was doing here, so far from his home planet, trading in this shadowy cave with a race that required five members just to cheat one Drazi.

Something . . . perverse must have compelled him to come to Chloris 5.

Finally they arrived at a mutually agreeable price. As Ni'im was preparing to leave, he asked—almost as an afterthought, "You guys haven't seen a Human-looking guy with a cowl around here by any chance, have you?"

The five conferred, then called in three others who happened to be passing outside the cave. The conference was animated, and finally, one of them said, "You must mean the wizard."

"That may be the one I seek. Perhaps he said his name was Galen?" Ni'im said, eagerly now.

"Yes. That's the one. He was by this way a few days ago. He's on an important mission, you know."

"Do you know where I can find him?" Ni'im asked.

"Alas, he left no forwarding address."

Ni'im had to be satisfied with that. Downcast, he left the arachnids, returned to his ship, and began to set the controls for his next jump. Then he sat a moment, to catch his breath.

And suddenly, he wasn't there anymore. It happened so suddenly he had no time in which to be startled. Simply, he was standing on a dark plain, with fires burning in the distance, and the silhouette of a ruined city in the background.

"Hello, Ni'im," a voice behind him said.

Ni'im whirled. There was Galen, his face half-concealed by a cowl.

"I was looking for you," Ni'im said. When Galen didn't respond, he continued. "I talked with my ancestors recently."

"It was an enlightening discussion, I hope."

"Quite so," Ni'im replied. "Look, what is it you want of me? Why are you haunting my dreams?"

"You have a destiny, a very important one. But before I explain myself, please, look around."

Ni'im looked around. He was, indeed, back on the dark plain that Galen had shown him earlier. But this time he noticed that it was pocked with numerous craters. Some force of incalculable destruction had hammered this place. Looking more closely, he saw that the plain was strewn with chunks of concrete, twisted pieces of steel, shattered glass, and a lot of other things he couldn't identify. It was as if some giant had brought the debris of a great city to this place and dumped it. It was either that, or—

"Is it possible," he asked in a low voice, "that a city once stood upon this site?"

Galen nodded. "This was once Teknead, foremost of the cities of Daltron 7."

"And someone destroyed it?"

"Along with everything else on the planet."

"But who could have done this? And what am I doing here?"

"You are not here," Galen said. "You are on your ship, and you are having a dream. As for who could have perpetrated this atrocity—you must go in person to Daltron 7 and find out."

"But what do I need to find out?"

"You must learn when the Dark Ones will return. And you must give that information to the others. But you must be very careful. Once you have what you need, you must get away fast, at the very first sign of danger."

"And then?"

"Then you will seek out the others."

Galen stooped and, picking up a stick, sketched three circles in the rubble. As Ni'im watched, faces filled the circles. There was a bearded, light-skinned Earther; a dark-skinned Earther; and a savage-looking, black-haired woman of a species unknown to him.

"And what happens after I find them?"

"They will know what to do," Galen said.

He made a sudden pass with his hand. Ni'im's vision grew dim. When he recovered, he was back on his ship.

—— chapter 30 ——

In her office on Babylon 5, Captain Lochley was having morning coffee at her desk. Garibaldi walked in, looking rumpled and grumpy. Lochley barely looked up.

"Good morning, Captain," Garibaldi said. He sat down near her and poured himself a coffee from the carafe.

"Mr. Garibaldi," Lochley said. "Sleep well?"

"Yeah," Garibaldi said. "Needed it, too. So where's the president?"

Lochley stared at him. "I thought he was with you."

"No," Garibaldi said. "When he didn't call, I figured he was gonna meet me here."

"That's odd," Lochley said.

She toggled her link.

Lieutenant Corwin answered, "On-line."

"Did you send President Sheridan a message reminding him about our meeting this morning?"

"Yes, ma'am. But he's been working and hasn't checked in."

"If you know he hasn't checked in, how do you know he's working?" she asked, suspicion growing in her voice.

"That's what the message says," Corwin said.

"Show me," Lochley ordered.

She and Garibaldi moved to the monitor, which lit up with Sheridan's face. There was something too happy, too innocent about the president's expression as he said, "Hello, this is the president. I'm dealing with affairs of state, and can't come to the link right now. At the chime, please leave a message and I'll get back to you at the earliest—"

Lochley toggled off the monitor. She and Garibaldi exchanged ominous looks.

Lochley said, "He wouldn't—"

"If he wanted to skip out," Garibaldi said, "he could. He knows all the ways in and out of here."

Lochley said, into the link, "Is the *White Star* still berthed outside?"

"Affirmative," Corwin said.

"Well, that's a relief," Garibaldi said.

"Wait . . ." Into the link, Lochley said, "Were there *any* departures during the night?"

"Just one," Corwin said. "The EarthForce destroyer *Charon*."

"Oh, hell," Garibaldi said.

He moved her arm around so he could speak into her link.

"Listen . . . I'm going to give you a frequency, and you get me on the line ASAP with Samuel Drake."

"Who?" Lochley asked.

—— *chapter 31* ——

And aboard the destroyer *Charon*, traveling through hyperspace, just before Garibaldi got onto the link, Sheridan was telephoning the selfsame Samuel Drake. Anderson and Dureena stood nearby.

"Samuel Drake, please," Sheridan said.

Drake's face appeared on the screen.

"Yes, Mr. President?"

"Mr. Drake, there has been a breach in security. Our communication frequency has been cracked, and Mr. Garibaldi believes that certain parties may use it to send you false or misleading information."

"I see," Drake said. "If I may ask, where is Mr. Garib—"

"Consequently," Sheridan continued, "you are *not* to accept any further messages unless they come in on this frequency. Lock everything else out of your system. Do not acknowledge, receive, or answer them for any reason. Is that understood, Drake?"

"Yes, sir," Drake responded.

"Good. I'm counting on you. We're en route and will be there shortly.

"End signal." Sheridan cut off Drake before he could reply.

Then he turned his attention to Anderson. "Have you talked to the rest of your crew?"

"I have," Anderson said. "They're all on board for this."

"And what about you? Are you sure you want to do this? You're going AWOL, risking your career . . ."

Anderson took his time before answering. Then he replied, "During the Civil War, we had a chance to join your side . . . We didn't, and we were wrong. When this . . . dream came to me, I didn't know if it was real or not. That's why we came.

"If you hadn't been here, I would've written the whole thing off as a delusion and moved on. But you *were* here, Earth *is* in danger . . . and this time I have every intention of being on the winning side. The crew feels the same way. We let you down once; we won't do it again."

Sheridan said, "Thank you, Captain. So . . . is everything ready?"

"I think so."

"Then we're in good shape."

Sheridan looked past Anderson to where Dureena was absently playing with a blade made of some dull red metal, with a curving surface like a Malay kris. Her glance up at him was still far from trusting.

Anderson noted it, and said to him quietly, "I see . . . And what does the phrase *in good shape* mean on the planet where *you* live?"

Sheridan shot him a look and left the bridge.

The *Charon* emerged from hyperspace and headed for the spacedock.

—— chapter 32 ——

Drake ran down the winding corridors of the interior of the spacedock, past the engine room that supplied the power for the dock's many duties, past the mess and storage facilities. He had only a few minutes before he had to report to Sheridan on *Excalibur*. But he knew that Cora had arrived from Babylon 5, and he couldn't wait to see her. She had to be in the oxygen regeneration area.

His footsteps made muffled pounding sounds as he ran down the final, long corridor leading to the oxygen regeneration area. He went through the double sealing doors and found himself in a tumbling mass of greenery. At the far end of the big room, he made out a slim figure in a red jumpsuit.

Cora!

He hugged her tightly to him, breathing in her fragrance. She responded with a smile and a kiss on his cheek.

"Oh, my dear," he said, breathless, "how happy I am to see you!"

Cora smiled radiantly. "Hello, Samuel. It's wonderful to see you. It's *all* wonderful. Look . . . look at this!"

161

She held out a purple and silver badge. Drake stared at it, uncomprehendingly.

"What is it?"

"Top security clearance! I needed it to get aboard the spacedock. How about that—little old me with a top security clearance! One of the guards almost saluted me!"

"That's really great," Drake said. Strangely, he found he was annoyed. She actually seemed more impressed by her silly clearance than at seeing him.

Then he reminded himself that she was young, very young. She'd need to grow into a proper appreciation of what was genuinely important. He would educate her . . .

She spoke up again, and asked him, "What's all the excitement about? So many people running around!"

"There's an official inspection coming up soon," he told her. "President Sheridan himself is on his way here, and I have to be prepared. But first, Cora, how are you? Isn't it wonderful that we—"

"I'm *great*," she replied brightly, cutting him off. "I can't believe how well my job is going. At first I was afraid of Professor Chapenton. He's in charge of our section, you know, and he's got this very stern look. But he's a dear, actually. And he says I'm doing good work! That's why they sent me here! And a good thing they did! Just *look* at these leaves!"

Drake looked at a mass of green in a big vat. "What about them?" he asked.

"Unmistakable signs of mold! Good thing they got me out here when they did! I've got an eye for details like this!"

Drake controlled his impatience with some difficulty. Cora could be very silly at times, chattering away
about inconsequential matters. If he weren't so sure
of her feelings toward him, he could almost think she
was more excited about her stupid job than about seeing him.

"Cora, please, there's something I want to tell you—"

"Oh, good! I have something to tell you, too. Wonderful news!"

"Really, what is it?"

"Rory sent me a package! All the way from Sioux
City—on Earth! You can't *imagine* the expense! I told
you about Rory, didn't I?"

Drake vaguely remembered her saying something
about some high school boy back home. A silly-sounding
fellow, one of those dim-witted jocks, with a letter in
some sport or another.

"Well, he sent me roses! They didn't hold up too
well, but they were definitely roses. And he sent me a
poem. Can you *imagine*, Rory writing a poem? I mean,
he's a business major."

"I can imagine it only with great difficulty," Drake
said. He was beginning to experience a curious detachment, as though all this weren't actually happening.
Detachment, and . . .

"And in this poem—this is the most wonderful
part—he *proposed*. Rory proposed to me! Can you *believe* it?"

Drake just stared. Detachment was the only thing he
had left now, his shield against the painful violence
of his feelings. Her words had shattered his delusions,

reminded him of who he was: Martian-born, someone no Earth girl could ever love.

Finally he found something to say. "I didn't know he was serious about you. You never said—"

"I know," Cora said. "That's because I never dreamed I had a chance. Oh, we went out a few times, and I helped him with his classwork. But after he moved away, and I got the job on Mars, I never imagined . . . And then *this*. I'm so happy, I don't know what to say."

Drake spoke carefully, reaching for a glimmer of hope. "A proposal in a poem—it might simply be poetic license—"

"But then he called all the way from Earth. It must have cost him the world! He called and proposed." She laughed. "It didn't rhyme this time, but I said yes anyhow."

"You accepted? But . . ."

"You think it was crazy? Oh, it wasn't, really. While we were separated, I realized I've loved Rory for years." She looked at Drake with her big blue eyes— eyes that he noticed for the first time were a little insipid. "Oh, Samuel, it's so good to have you to talk to. You're like a brother to me—a brother I never had."

"I'm glad you feel that way," Drake said, feeling like death inside. Stiffly, he forced himself to speak anyway. "My sincere congratulations, Cora. But now you'll have to excuse me. I'm wanted on *Excalibur*." He started to walk away.

"I'll see you before I leave, won't I?"

"Oh, I'm sure. I mean, I'll try. But if not, there's always E-mail." He hurried away, not trusting himself to say another word, only knowing that his dream had

been shattered, shot down before it even had a chance
to fly.

All that lay ahead of him now was a chance to show
them all who he was, and how little they had reckoned
with Samuel Drake.

—— *chapter 33* ——

Once again, Sheridan was impressed by the sheer size of *Excalibur*, the impression it gave of brute strength. But he was reacting to more than the machine. He *liked* this ship. It gave him a rare feeling of correctness. Something about the proportions, perhaps, or the busy vistas of corridors, compartments, rooms, multilevel spaces . . . it gave him a feeling he had experienced looking at ancient architecture—the Parthenon of Athens, the Colosseum of Rome, the Second Imperial Palace on Minbar—a feeling of beauty combined with rightness.

The *Excalibur*, he knew, was a classic. And that it was a classic of the future made it all the more rare, and endearing. Without quite knowing how it had happened, Sheridan had already formed a strong attachment to this ship.

Drake came down the corridor, moving toward him on the run, an odd look of panic on his face.

"Mr. President, I'm sorry, we're not ready. We didn't think you'd be coming back so soon, I—"

"Quite all right," Sheridan said. "Drake, this is Captain Anderson and Dureena Nafeel. I brought them along to see the tour."

"I see," Drake said. "This is quite irregular. They haven't been cleared—"

"And some of their friends," Sheridan continued.

The EarthForce personnel from *Charon* came pouring around the corner behind him, in full battle gear and armed to the teeth. They moved past Drake without even seeming to notice him.

"No, no!" Drake said in alarm. "This is out of— We don't have the facilities for— You can't go in there!" he called after the last of them.

"Of course they can," Sheridan said, putting an arm around Drake's shoulders and firmly moving him toward the bridge. "Now, tell me that part again about how the systems were designed to use standard EarthForce controls. That means there won't be much of a curve involved in learning to run this thing, am I right?"

"Well, yes," Drake said. "But—"

Dureena and Anderson watched as Drake let Sheridan guide him away. They exchanged glances: Sheridan was handling this man well.

But why did Drake need such handling?

chapter 34

Garibaldi had lost no time, once he'd discovered that Sheridan had left without telling anyone, using the destroyer *Charon* to slip away unnoticed. He didn't know what in hell was going on, but he was determined to find out, and to be in on it.

His thoughts ranged widely through possibilities. Maybe Sheridan finally *had* gone around the bend, turned completely crazy. He'd always had that imperious need to act on his own thinking, no matter what anyone else thought. And Garibaldi thought back, remembered when Sheridan had cut all ties between Babylon 5 and Earth.

At the time, Garibaldi had fought Sheridan tooth and nail, accused him of acting like a man with a messiah complex. Garibaldi subsequently discovered that he himself was being telepathically influenced by that little Hitler, Bester, but that didn't change the inescapable fact that Sheridan had the habit of acting on his own grandiosity.

Of course, there was the possibility that Sheridan wasn't crazy at all, that he knew something no one else knew. Something he couldn't reveal at this time.

Garibaldi didn't know which was true. But there might be a way of finding out.

He was standing beside a communication monitor, with a Minbari Ranger working the controls, trying frantically to get through to Drake.

"I repeat, this is White Star 90 to Samuel Drake . . . Please respond."

Finally the Ranger said, "No good, sir. They're blocking us."

"Damn!" Garibaldi responded.

"It doesn't make any sense, sir," the Ranger said. "Why would he go back there? It's not as if he's going to steal the new ships, or any—" He stopped, reacting to Garibaldi's look. "He wouldn't!"

"If he thought he needed them," Garibaldi said, "and he thought he was right . . . he'd do it."

—— *chapter 35* ——

The bridge of the *Excalibur* was a beehive of purposeful activity. The men and women of Earth-Force were moving to stations similar to those they had known on other ships, checking out instruments that, if not identical to those they had operated, were at least similar enough to let them do their jobs.

Here and there were quick, low-voiced conversations as personnel checked out momentarily baffling situations with their friends and colleagues and came up with quick, efficient solutions.

Sheridan was proud. He had taken half of *Charon*'s complement with him to *Excalibur*. The other half were with Anderson aboard the *Victory*. The two men were in constant radio communication. Dureena watched all this without comment, but couldn't help but be impressed by the purposeful air of these soldiers.

Anderson reported in. "*Victory* to *Excalibur*. We're ready to go."

In response, Sheridan addressed his bridge crew. "Arm gravitational engines. Ahead one quarter."

The navigation officer looked up. "Unable to comply. We're still locked into spacedock."

"Well . . . release the locks."

"We don't have the codes, sir."

Sheridan nodded. He looked at a console alongside the ship, touched a panel. On *Excalibur*'s great, smooth, shining flank, a gun turned in its turret, took aim at a locking mechanism that was holding the ship in place. On *Victory*, Anderson followed suit.

The guns on the two ships fired almost simultaneously. The locks flew apart in a welter of metal shards. The ships were free of the dry dock.

"Problem solved," Sheridan said. "Set course for . . ."

He paused, considered. Where *were* they going?

Then he remembered his conversation with Galen, remembered the techno-mage saying, "Unless you act, Earth may suffer the fate of Daltron 7."

Sheridan turned to the Ranger who was stationed at the control module. "Set course for Daltron 7."

If the Ranger considered this an odd request, he didn't indicate it. He punched in the settings.

Sheridan smiled as the great ship glided away from the spacedock, followed closely by *Victory*. He loved this ship!

He said, "Prepare to jump to hyperspace." He waited a moment, then, "Jump!"

The two ships leapt into the glowing oval of hyperspace as it opened up in front of them.

chapter 36

The planet rotated slowly under a haze of dark clouds. Near it, two jump points formed up. *Excalibur* and *Victory* came flashing out of hyperspace.

On *Excalibur*'s bridge, John Sheridan began studying the planet below.

Nearby, the Ranger at the navigation console announced, "Daltron 7, dead ahead, sir."

"Can't be," Sheridan said. "The reference table on Daltron 7 describes this as the next best thing to paradise. Clear skies, warm temperatures . . ."

He turned to the main display console.

"Ship . . . environmental analysis of planet."

A detailed analysis of Daltron 7 sprang up on the display.

The computer said, "Nitrogen-oxygen atmosphere, in proportions dangerous for Human life-forms. High degree of carbon ash and particulate matter in upper atmosphere indicative of surface eruptions. Surface temperature fourteen degrees Fahrenheit. Temperature of planetary core far below normal levels. Anomalous surface details."

"What kind of surface details?" Sheridan asked.

The display shifted to a computer enhancement. It gradually peeled away the cloud layer to reveal thousands of craters all over the planet's surface. Dureena saw this and came up alongside Sheridan.

She said, "This—this is what they did to my world."

"But that doesn't make any sense," Sheridan said. "Daltron 7 was well outside the war zone. Besides, it's been six years since the war . . . An attack here, even this far off the main routes, we would've heard about it by now."

He touched the console. "Ship . . . have you picked up any life-forms? Anything at all?"

"Negative on life-forms," the computer voice responded. "Picking up one power source."

"Identify the power source," Sheridan said.

The computer complied. "Distress signal of Drazi origin."

"Fire up a shuttle," Sheridan said, "then tell Captain Anderson to do the same. We're going down there."

He turned on his heel and marched off. Dureena looked once again at the image with horrified familiarity. Then she followed.

—— *chapter 37* ——

Excalibur and *Victory* hovered above Daltron 7. Again almost simultaneously, two atmospheric shuttles emerged from their launching bays. They arced away from their command ships, toward the planet below.

Aboard the shuttle from *Excalibur*, John Sheridan and Dureena Nafeel sat in seats behind the pilot. To the rear, on facing benches, an EarthForce guard detail sat in full battle gear, weapons at the ready. Sheridan watched pensively as they spiraled down into Daltron 7's murky atmosphere.

The shuttle was buffeted by the inescapable strong winds that dominated the upper atmosphere, but the pilot controlled the craft, making a safe descent. The launch came out of the murky upper atmosphere, and suddenly there was a landscape stretching below them.

It was a nightmare scene. Once-fertile land had been subjected to an endless rain of heat and explosives, leaving everything a wasteland. During the attack, some deep-burrowing missiles must have penetrated to the planet's core, for there were great plains of shiny black volcanic material. It was apparent that underground explosions of stupendous force had occurred, literally blowing out the inside of the planet.

In the far distance, Sheridan could see a mountain. Closer, there were the shattered remains of a city. The place literally had been turned inside out. Masonry blocks and steel girders were scattered like jackstraws. In the city's center, a huge hole had been gouged into the ground.

"This is it," Sheridan said. "This is the place I saw in my dream." In his nightmare.

Once on the ground, Sheridan led them to the spot he had stood on before. He was wearing a parka from the launch, breather equipment that covered the lower half of his face, and he was armed. Dureena and Anderson, following behind him, were similarly clad and equipped.

Anderson had a tracking device, which he clutched in one gloved hand. He walked slowly, sweeping it from side to side, looking for the distress signal they had detected from shipboard.

The device's beeping grew louder, increased in frequency as he moved in the right direction. Then, in front of a long mound of dirt, it seemed to explode into a constant chatter.

Anderson gestured to the others, then knelt down beside the mound and began gently brushing away the dirt. The soil was light and easy to work. Soon his efforts were rewarded as he brought up a palm-sized beacon transmitter.

"I've found the beacon!" Anderson said. He searched deeper into the mound. "And something else."

As Sheridan and Dureena gathered around, Anderson brushed away more dirt, revealing a hand . . . a Drazi hand.

Sheridan knelt down and studied the face as Anderson uncovered it.

Anderson straightened up. "Is this the Drazi we were supposed to meet up with?"

Sheridan bent and looked intently at the face. "It's hard to be sure, but . . . yes, it looks like him."

"Somebody got to him before we could," Anderson said. "I want the body searched. He might have left a note, anything that might tell us what happened here."

Sheridan nodded to the guards, who came forward and started to work unburying the body. Dureena watched intently. Meanwhile one of the guards brought a comp-pad to Anderson, who studied the report.

"What is it?" Sheridan asked.

Anderson said, "I told my crew to do a more detailed surface analysis, scan the planetary core, and back-check the records, see if anyone reported what happened here."

"And?" Dureena asked.

"Look," Anderson said, "I wasn't involved in the Shadow War, you were . . . So I didn't see these death-clouds. But . . . Are you sure this was done by a Shadow Planet Killer?"

"Positive," Sheridan said. "Nothing else leaves a pattern of craters like we saw from above. I've never seen anything like it before or since."

"And that was six years ago, right?"

"Correct. Then the Shadows left and took it with them."

"Then we've got a serious problem on our hands, Mr. President . . . Because if what I'm seeing here is correct, all this happened just over a week ago."

Sheridan and Dureena were silent for a few moments, as the full implication of Anderson's information sank in. Dureena's face was unreadable. Sheridan was obviously thinking, *Oh, no, not again!*

Finally, Sheridan broke the silence. "The Drazi looks like he's only been dead a few days. He might have seen something."

Anderson called to the guards, "Anything on the body?"

The guards shook their heads.

"So it's a dead end," Sheridan said with disappointment.

"Not necessarily," Dureena interjected. She walked over to the body, knelt down on one knee, and studied it intently. Then she slid a large knife out of her belt.

"Wait a minute," Sheridan protested. "What're you—"

Before Sheridan or Anderson could react, she drove the blade deep into the Drazi's body, in the left armpit. She rooted around with it for a moment, then felt something with the blade. She worked it to form an opening, then reached into the white-rimmed gap and pulled out a data crystal. She stood up again, walked over to Anderson, and put it in his hand.

She said, "Male Drazi have a . . . pouch under their left arm. It's covered by a skin flap. You can't see it if you don't know what to look for. Drazi smugglers use it to transport small items into other parts of space. If he was in trouble and he wanted to make sure the crystal wouldn't be found, this was the logical place to hide it."

Without waiting for their reaction, she walked off. Sheridan had the feeling that this was all very normal for her.

Anderson turned the data crystal over in his hand. "I didn't know Drazi had a skin pouch under their arms."

Sheridan looked vaguely pained. "That's not a pouch. Well, not technically. That's . . . their reproductive area."

He also walked off.

Anderson looked at the still-wet data crystal in his hand. Although he was a hardened captain, he thought this was gross.

He called after Sheridan, "Did you *have* to tell me that?"

Then, to Dureena, "Hey, lady . . . Dureena . . . Listen, just for the record, the only valuable thing I carry with me is my watch. I want you to know that—just in case this *ever* comes up in the future. Okay?"

After that, they finished up their work quickly. Soon, Sheridan was sitting beside Dureena back on the *Excalibur* shuttle. Through the port they could see *Victory*'s shuttle, with Anderson aboard.

Sheridan said to Dureena, "You did well back there. But I can't help wondering how someone who's supposedly just a pickpocket knows so much about smuggling and alien life-forms."

"I'm more concerned with what you said," Dureena replied evasively. "You said you beat the Shadows. You said they went away and took their weapons with them, the weapons they used to murder my people." She looked him straight in the eye. "You were wrong."

"We knew they'd hidden some of their weapons on other planets, as a safety measure, but we didn't think anyone else would know where they were, or how to use them. But the Drakh would know . . . they probably helped build the damn things."

"So you have had this problem before?"

"Leftover Shadow tech? Yeah, a few times, but nothing this major."

"And what happened?" Dureena asked.

"We got our butts kicked, every time," Sheridan said.

"Ah," Dureena said. "Perhaps I should shoot myself now, and save myself a great deal of time and trouble."

She thought for a moment. "No, that would be selfish. As their greatest enemy, they would have terrible plans for you if we do not stop them." She nodded to herself. "Agreed. First I will shoot you, *then* I will shoot me. I would consider it a public service."

"I'm honored," Sheridan said wryly.

"You're welcome," Dureena said.

—— *chapter 38* ——

Garibaldi had returned to the construction dock. The place was well lit. There were spotlights on the various gantries and towers, lights on the toolsheds and staging areas. There were even banners, bunting, and other decorative splashes, all Drake's preparations for the ceremony that would inaugurate the two newest ships in the EarthForce fleet. It looked like a place that was all dressed up for a party, but the guests weren't there.

Excalibur and *Victory* were gone, taken off, as Drake had told Garibaldi in exhaustive detail, on whatever madcap adventure President Sheridan had seen fit to take them.

"It was terrible, Mr. Garibaldi, simply terrible," Drake said, finishing up his dramatic tale of how Sheridan and Anderson had come down in *Charon* and seized the two prototypes without so much as a by-your-leave.

Garibaldi nodded absently. They were in the *White Star*'s dining room. Drake was sitting and talking, and Garibaldi was prowling around, half listening, drawing his own conclusions.

Drake went on, "Sheridan was like . . . like a madman. He just broke in here and stole the prototypes.

You should've seen the look in his eyes . . . I was sure he was going to kill me."

"Did he say where he was going?" Garibaldi asked. He stopped his pacing for a moment.

"No . . . But he was in a big hurry to get there, I can tell you that."

"Then what the hell— Wait a minute. He wanted me to check out a planet out on the deep range. What was the name . . . Dal . . . Daltron 7."

"Is that where he went?" Drake asked anxiously.

"I don't know," Garibaldi said. "But it's a lead, and the only one we've got at the moment. I'll have you shuttled back over—"

"No!" Drake said. "After what I've been through, I want to be there when you catch up with him. Besides, those two prototypes are my babies, Mr. Garibaldi. I should be there when they're found."

"All right. I think they've got a spare bunk room downstairs. Check with Lennok and see what he can do for you."

Drake left the dining room as Garibaldi touched a com system.

"Garibaldi to bridge. Set course for Daltron 7. Best speed."

The *White Star* turned within its own length and raced away, opening up a jump point as it went.

—— chapter 39 ——

Anderson's quarters aboard the *Victory* were identical to Sheridan's. He was sitting there, studying a photograph in a framed case. It showed a beautiful, dark-skinned woman with thick, crinkled hair that was tied back in a club. There was a little girl beside her, and she was wearing a joyous grin.

A light came on at the console. His first officer's voice announced, "Captain, we've managed to get a clear signal through to Earth."

"Good," Anderson replied. "Put it through."

The woman from the photograph appeared on the screen, looking a few years older but no less attractive.

"Hello, Lynne," Anderson said, his voice husky.

"Leonard? My God, where have you been? They've been calling, saying you've deserted—"

"I haven't deserted," Anderson said reassuringly. "Let's just say I've . . . been transferred by a higher power. I can't really talk about it on an open channel. I just wanted to see if you and Sarah were okay."

"We're fine," Lynne said. "I'm just worried about you."

"I'll be fine," Anderson said. "You know how I am."

Just then Sarah, impudent and beautiful, jumped up into the camera range.

Anderson said, "Hey, Sarah . . . You okay?"

"I'm okay," Sarah said. A serious expression crossed her face, and she added, "But I had a bad dream. I dreamed I was being chased by monsters and they ate me."

Lynne said, "She's saying she won't go to sleep tonight because the monsters will get her."

"They will!" Sarah insisted.

"No, they won't, Sarah," Anderson said gently. "I'll make sure of that. Doesn't matter where I am, far or near, I'll keep the monsters away from you, Sarah. I promise."

The first officer's voice broke in on the conversation. "Captain, they've got the Drazi data crystal decoded."

"On my way," Anderson responded. To Sarah he said, "I have to go. Now get some sleep, Sarah.

"I love you, Lynne."

"I love you, too, Leonard," Lynne said.

──── chapter 40 ────

Aboard *Excalibur*, Sheridan was playing the recording the Drazi had made on the data crystal. The image was broken by static, apparently the result of damage to the crystal itself. Beside him, Dureena was also watching with great interest.

The image showed Ni'im in a standard Drazi cockpit. He was saying, ". . . and the dreams spoke to me. They called to me, to come to this place. When I arrived, the destroyer was here. I sent a probe in to examine it. It looked like this."

Ni'im's image faded out and changed to a distant view of Daltron 7, apparently taken as Ni'im was coming in for a landing. It showed a beautiful world, green and blue like Earth, the sky dotted here and there with small clouds. Creeping in from the edges, though, from the depths of space, there was a great cloud, a sinister shadow that seemed made of sentient matter.

It descended slowly, sending out tendrils of darkness that reached toward the planet. As they watched, the entire sky was engulfed. Through the darkness, flashes of brilliant light could be seen. Each lasted no longer than a moment, coming from the dense mass that hovered above the surface of the planet. Nonetheless, there were many of these flashes. The view shifted, offering close-ups of the planet surface. That, too, was lit luridly by the continual flashing, which seemed like a frenzy of fireflies gone mad. The planet seemed to shudder as it took multiple hits. Great sore spots opened in its surface. Cities and farmland disappeared under the bombardment and were replaced by gaping craters as raw as wounds on a leper's skin.

Dureena seemed intoxicated by the image, staring at it wide-eyed. Watching her eyes, Sheridan was sure she was reliving the destruction of her own planet. His heart went out to her.

He said, "Perhaps you should—"

"No, I am all right. But promise that someday you will let me kill that thing."

"It isn't alive," Sheridan said.

"No?" Then she turned back to the screen, because the Drazi was speaking again.

"It is a terrible thing," Ni'im said. "A slayer of worlds. An echo of the darkness we thought had finally left us."

More scenes of the destruction of Daltron 7 followed.

When the image focused once more on Ni'im, he said, "When it was finished, the others who were with it took it away. I followed them to this location."

There flashed on the screen a series of triangulation grids and locater figures.

"I would have investigated further," Ni'im went on, "but there were too many. So I am returning to Daltron 7 to see if there are any who can be saved. Then I will wait for the others in my dream to come. With luck, the Dark Ones will not find me before they can arrive.

"End message."

The image broke up in static. Sheridan toggled the device, turning off the recording. He and Dureena stared at the blank screen, neither saying anything.

—— *chapter 41* ——

From the bridge on *Victory*, Anderson was trying anxiously to get through to Sheridan on *Excalibur*. Finally he succeeded.

"Mr. President—"

Sheridan seemed to come back from a long way away. "Yes, yes, Captain, what is it?"

"Check your long-range scanners," Anderson said. "We've got company."

Sheridan snapped at a crew member, "Show me."

On both ships, the display changed to a distant shot that revealed four Drakh warships. They were still too far away for the scanners to pick up much detail, but their shapes were unmistakable, and evoked a terror reminiscent of an ancestral memory. This was one of the faces of evil, and even at a glance it could be identified as such.

The first officer said, "Are those Drakh?"

Anderson said, "They're either Drakh or the weirdest-looking pizza delivery trucks I've ever seen. And we're a *long* way from pepperoni, son."

* * *

On *Excalibur*, Sheridan asked communications, "Have they taken any hostile action yet?"

"Negative, sir," communications replied. "Picking up scanners; I think they're trying to figure out who and what we are."

To Anderson, Sheridan said, "They don't recognize our ships. Good, that's what I was counting on. Let them get closer, Captain."

"Understood," Anderson said.

"We'll lay low until we can see right down their gun ports." He turned to his first officer. "Keep a finger on the trigger. If they do anything suspicious, knock 'em down."

After a few moments, communications reported to Sheridan, "Sir, getting a transmission from the Drakh ships."

"Receive transmission," Sheridan ordered. "But do *not* respond, video or audio. If we can get a look at them without them getting a look at us—"

"Message coming through," communications said. "Message is in Interlac, using an autotranslation system."

And then the display lit up with a full image of a Drakh ship, the first they had seen close up.

Once you saw a Drakh ship, you never forgot it. It had a central mass like an elongated egg and, surrounding that, long, building members that suggested insect legs. It was a shape born of an alien nightmare, a shape whose very proportions spoke of an unnatural evil. Shapes like this seemed to stimulate some dim center in Humankind's collective mind, where evil was stored, as a frog might store in its ancestral memory the supple flicking movement of an attacking snake.

"You have no business in this area," the Drakh voice said, and somehow the automatic machine translation conveyed some hint of the sinister nature of the creature speaking. "Who are you? Identify yourself."

"The voice of the enemy," Sheridan remarked to his crew. "Don't respond."

"Wait," Dureena said. "I have a better idea."

She turned to communications. "Send them a reply in Interlac, audio only. Tell them, 'We came to attend to our enemies, but found that someone had already dealt with them. We were hoping to thank whoever was responsible.' "

She turned to Sheridan. "Doesn't matter how powerful they are, they're going to need all the allies they can get. Let's see if we can convince them we could be such an ally and see what happens."

Communications looked at Sheridan; the decision was his to make. It was a chain-of-command thing. Sheridan nodded. The idea sounded good to him.

"Send it," Sheridan said.

Communications acknowledged, selected the translating program, and sent the message off.

They waited.

Suddenly the room was wracked by a high-pitched sound from the com system. It was like nails on a blackboard, loud as a siren. The com officer shut it off as fast as he could.

"What was that?" Sheridan asked.

"Transmission coming in on the Drakh frequency.

Extremely powerful, tachyon-enhanced. It definitely came from outside the system. No way to trace it."

"You're sure it was meant for them?"

"Positive."

"What's their position?" Sheridan asked.

The navigation officer said, "They've stopped their approach. Holding steady."

"I don't like this," Sheridan said. "Any further communication?"

"No, sir," communications said.

"Damn," Sheridan said. "I *knew* this was too easy. All hands man battle stations. Communications, start jamming their transmissions. Navigation, give me full power to the engines as soon as—"

The navigation officer cried, "There they go!"

In the view screen they could see the four Drakh ships break into two groups. One pair raced toward Sheridan's position, the other broke away at a right angle.

Sheridan said, "Anderson, you take the two on approach, I'll go after the others!"

"We've got 'em!" Anderson replied. He checked his console. "Forward guns, prepare to fire!"

"Aye, sir," control said. "Targets coming into range."

The *Victory*'s first officer announced, "Enemy ships are locking on, firing!"

In the next moment, Anderson was looking straight down the path of incoming fire. Beam projection for the most part, propagating along the line of attack faster than the eye could see. Anderson barely had time to think, *Now we'll see how good this new ship is at preserving herself.*

Then the ship was rocked, and for a moment the lights dimmed. *Victory* had taken dead-on hits. But it was apparent a moment later that the hits had been deflected off the hull, dispersed in a rainbow of diffusion.

"Damage report!" Anderson said.

"Minor damage to outer decks," the first officer responded. "The hull appears to be refracting away most of the energy."

"Outstanding!" Anderson said. "Weapons control— *fire!*"

The *Victory*'s big forward guns let fly in a soundless bellow. One of the Drakh ships managed to get out of the line of fire, fluttering away like a wounded moth before it could pick up speed again. The other one, trying the same tactic, zigged the wrong way. It was caught full in a blast and was obliterated.

Now it was the other Drakh ship that Anderson was concerned with.

"She's making a run for it!" the first officer said.

"Stay with her," Anderson instructed.

The *Victory* wheeled and set off after the Drakh.

Excalibur, moving in the opposite direction, was in pursuit of the remaining two Drakh ships.

There was silence on the bridge as the stern chase continued. Sheridan had the impression, from visual evidence, that they were gaining.

"Distance to target!" he demanded.

The navigation officer responded, "Two thousand miles to optimum firing range, closing fast. Sixty seconds to target acquisition. Fifty-five. Fifty . . ."

Just then something came up on the display, and

looking out the window, Sheridan saw something he couldn't identify.

"What in hell is that?" Sheridan asked.

Several of the crew crowded to the window. The spray of stars that covered the sky, like points of light of differing sizes, had been interrupted, broken by an area, kilometers across, where the stars simply didn't seem to shine. Something was in the way—a perfectly square something that blocked out everything in view. The Drakh ships were running toward that void.

The navigator reported, "We're getting nothing on the scanners. It's like a null field out there, absorbing everything, even the light."

"And those ships are headed right for it. How long before they enter the field?"

"Thirty seconds," the navigator said.

"Prepare to fire main guns," Sheridan said.

"Warning!" control said. "If main guns are fired—"

"I know," Sheridan said. "Stand by to fire. Stand by . . . Fire!"

The lights went dim as *Excalibur*'s main armament erupted in a stupendous explosion. If Sheridan had had any lingering doubt as to the efficacy of his main weapons, it was dispelled now. The energy bolt, by far the largest he had ever delivered, hit between the two Drakh ships. The resulting explosion vaporized them both.

Milliseconds after the blow had been delivered, all the lights on *Excalibur* went out, then came faintly back on as power began rebuilding.

"Temporary power loss," navigation reported. "Fifty seconds to rebuild."

"Distance to null field?" Sheridan asked.

"Ten seconds," navigation replied.

Sheridan stood in front of the port, waiting. *Excalibur* was heading straight for the center of the null field. It loomed ahead of the ship, an apparently solid obstacle, black, impervious-looking.

—— chapter 42 ——

They were hurtling full speed ahead into a gigantic black object in space, but there was no time to panic, even if someone had wanted to.

Dureena's expression was characteristically unreadable as she watched the ship rushing toward the vast darkness. The navigation officer was making a low sound in the back of his throat, and seemed to be unaware he was doing it.

The black wall loomed up ahead of them, given apparent curvature by the speed they were traveling and the angle at which they were encountering it. Sheridan braced, as did the others, as they plunged into it, expecting, perhaps, an impact, a moment of explosion, after which the ship would be broken down to its constituent elements.

No such thing happened. There was no impact, no discernible change. One moment they were in normal space, the next moment they were within the null field. It was darker than space had ever been, with a darkness that seemed to suck away any source of light, leaving only the black nothingness behind.

A thought occurred to Sheridan. He said aloud,

"Navigation . . . just an idle thought. Does this location by any chance correspond to the one mentioned in the Drazi recording?"

"Yes, sir," the navigation officer replied.

Sheridan nodded, waiting as the ship tore through the darkness. He didn't know what to expect, there in that gloom in which the only sources of illumination were the pinpoint lights from the bridge consoles.

He wondered how deep this thing was, how long it would take them to get through it. He remembered stories he had heard about black holes. Might this be one of them? In that case, they were destined to be in here forever, for nothing escaped the event horizon of a black hole.

But he didn't think this was a black hole. He'd never heard of anyone, not even a First One, being able to tow a black hole around with him. What else, then? Something anomalous, perhaps, like hyperspace, but with its own peculiar properties . . . More likely, it was a masking device developed by the Drakhs, probably using a technology they had picked up from the Shadows . . .

Suddenly, they were out the other side, and Sheridan was looking at the sight he had half expected all along.

Thousands of Drakh ships, arrayed in rows like beads on a lattice, were moving in an orderly, military fashion, in the process of entering something he'd never seen before: a movable jumpgate, evidently a temporary structure, held in place by a massive spider-like structure.

* * *

Anderson's crew was gripped in a state of controlled tension as the *Victory* crept up to the edge of the null field. Firing its forward thrusters, the ship stopped.

Anderson stared at the thing in front of him. It was like a huge wall covering space like an entrance into some futuristic hell.

"Are you sure they went in there?" he asked.

"Aye, sir," the first officer responded. "But we can't read anything beyond the null field."

"What the hell is it?" Anderson said, half to himself.

Then his eyes picked up a flash of light, and he saw something coming directly at his ship. His reaction was instantaneous.

"Hard to starboard! Right now!"

His well-trained crew responded without question, socking the engines up to high gain—not a generally approved maneuver but, given the circumstances, the only thing to do. The ship skidded to the side.

That was just as well, because an instant later, *Excalibur* came blasting back through, passing within yards of *Victory* and taking hits from half a dozen or more pursuing Drakh ships. Sheridan's ship was returning fire with its rear-mounted guns. *Excalibur* passed so closely that Anderson was sure he saw Sheridan's face in a forward view port, saw his mouth working, and could guess what the president's words were. "Get out of my way!"

And then they were past. A moment later, the pursuing Drakh were past him, too.

Anderson shouted, "Come about! Rear guns, fire! *Excalibur*, what happened?"

Sheridan's voice responded over the comlink. "The

fleet's on the move. All of 'em! They've sent the only ships they could spare after us!"

Sheridan's voice was lost for a moment as heavy noises on the com showed a hit had been taken. Then he came back on.

"Listen, Captain," Sheridan said, "I don't think these ships are jump-capable. I have a plan."

"What is it?" Anderson asked.

"Run like hell," Sheridan said, "and hope they're not fast enough to follow us into the jump point before it closes."

His voice grew fainter as he turned away from the com to address his own men. He said, "Prepare to jump."

"Standing by!" his navigation officer responded.

"Jump!" Sheridan ordered.

An instant later, *Excalibur* was into the jump point. The Drakh ships pursuing him had poured everything on but hadn't reached *Excalibur* before the point closed, destroying half of them.

Anderson, too, was commanding, "Jump!" His own jump point formed up. Ahead of it, a number of Drakh ships, which had turned to intercept *Victory*, were caught on the other side of the jump point and obliterated.

Excalibur and *Victory* shot side by side through hyperspace, two masses of machined metal hurtling along the mysterious shortcut that was the essence of hyperspace.

The question was, where were the Drakh?

"Are you picking up the enemy fleet?" Sheridan asked his navigation officer.

"Aye, sir. They're riding the primary hyperspace

beacon in this area. Ten thousand miles ahead of us, moving fast."

Sheridan nodded. "Take us off the hyperspace beacon. We'll try to slip past them. They can move only as fast as their slowest ship . . . so we've got an edge on them. Put us on a course for Earth, maximum burn. And get me Captain Lochley at Babylon 5."

── *chapter 43* ──

In Lochley's office, the captain was working at her desk when a call came through.

"Captain," Corwin said, "call coming in for you. It's from President Sheridan."

"Put him through," Lochley replied instantly. She had been worried about Sheridan. Although she admired the president more than any other man she knew, she actually had begun to question his sanity. It wouldn't be the first time a great man had become unhinged when faced with the paranoia that so often accompanies high office.

Sheridan's first words did nothing to ease her mind.

"Mr. President," she said, "I'm glad you finally decided to check in. We've been worried about—"

Sheridan interrupted, "Well, you've got good reason to be worried. I'm about three hours ahead of a Drakh assault fleet headed right for Earth. And Captain . . . they've got a Shadow Planet Killer with them."

"I see," Lochley said, remaining calm. A great sense of pity flooded her mind. That this should be happening to Sheridan, of all people!

She continued carefully, "Well, perhaps if you were

to stop off here on your way, we could discuss this a little—"

"Damn it, Captain," Sheridan said, "I know how this sounds, but it's true. Now I've contacted Delenn, and she's calling in as many Alliance ships as she can get on this kind of short notice. But that won't be enough. We need a full-scale mobilization back home."

"Earth isn't going to scramble every ship they've got just because I tell them to."

"Then you'll have to be more persuasive."

"Why me?"

"Because you're still part of EarthGov. Besides, they're still a little wary of me, given what happened last time I brought a fleet into Earth space. Captain Anderson doesn't have the clout to do it, and since he went AWOL to join us, his word won't count for a lot."

"You're asking the impossible," Lochley said flatly.

"Then I'm asking the right person. Elizabeth, if you've ever believed me, if you've ever trusted me . . . trust me now. We've dealt with a lot of issues over the years—when we were married, when you first arrived on Babylon 5—but trust has never been an issue.

"You haven't seen what a deathcloud can do. I have. It'll wipe out all life on Earth unless we stop it. Hell, I don't even know if it *can* be stopped. All I know is that we have to try."

Sheridan's face was totally in earnest. And although she was conflicted, she nodded.

"All right . . . I'll do what I can."

"Thanks," Sheridan said.

The screen went black. Lochley sat in front of it a moment longer, biting her lip, thinking furiously.

Then she said, "Lochley to C&C."

"C&C on-line."

She spoke with reluctance, but with decision. "Activate Gold Channel one. Put me through to EarthDome, President Susanna Luchenko's office."

"Captain," Corwin said, "it's three in the morning back there."

"I know, I know." She shook her head, as amazed at herself as at the situation. "I always knew I'd get court-martialed for something someday. Might as well get it over with now."

—— chapter 44 ——

Garibaldi came to the bridge of the *White Star* even as a Minbari Ranger approached him, comp-pad in hand.

"What's up?" Garibaldi asked.

"Something odd," the Ranger said. "We had an anomaly in the communications system turn up on a routine check. A sustained, coded message was routed through the StellarCom system. It even tapped into the main power system to boost the signal far beyond usual."

Garibaldi grunted. "Somebody must've really wanted to call home."

"No," the Minbari Ranger said, "I don't think—"

Just then the near console *breep*ed. The Ranger checked it.

"Incoming signal from President Sheridan."

"Put it on the screen," Garibaldi said.

Sheridan's image sprang up on the main viewer.

"Michael . . . the balloon's gone up. We've got an attack fleet heading for Earth. And they've got a Shadow Planet Killer."

Garibaldi tried—and failed—to hide his skepticism.

"How do you know they're heading for Earth? Another dream?"

"Yes," Sheridan said, "but more than that. Look at the timing, Michael. It's the fifth anniversary of the Alliance, which constitutes the primary threat to the Drakh and whatever plans they have for the future. The Alliance was born because Humans got into the Shadow War. Can you think of a better target?

"Look, I don't want to argue; I just wanted to warn you because I think the Drakh know we're on to them."

"Well," Garibaldi said, "if there's a leak, you may want to look close to home." He looked up and nodded as Drake came onto the bridge. "I just got word from Babylon 5 a little while ago: turns out the woman who joined you is a member of the Thieves' Guild, an organization of con men, crooks, extortionists, you name it. She's got a record as long as your arm, and I wouldn't trust her any farther than that."

Sheridan, on *Excalibur*, turned to Dureena. "Is this true?" When she nodded, he said, "Why didn't you tell me?"

Dureena said, "There's no sense in belonging to a secret group if you tell everyone about it. But if I were your leak, I would be very stupid, since I could have been killed alongside you."

Garibaldi had been monitoring the conversation. "Killed how?"

Sheridan supplied the answer. "We were being approached by four Drakh ships trying to make contact. Then suddenly they just attacked. They knew who we were. They recognized our ships."

"That's not possible," Garibaldi said. "Nobody's seen that design before. They couldn't have known."

"That's my point," Sheridan said. "They attacked right after receiving an extremely powerful transmission. Someone told them who we were, Michael. Somebody knew where we had gone, and identified our ships."

"But that—"

Garibaldi stopped in midsentence. A sudden realization came to his mind.

"This transmission . . . when did it come through?"

"About sixteen hundred hours GST."

"That's about the same time that—"

His words were cut off by the sound of a phased plasma gun firing up right behind his head.

Garibaldi continued calmly, "I think we've found the leak, Mr. President. I'll have to call you back."

"Michael—"

The transmission blipped off as Garibaldi turned to face his assailant. Drake was pointing the gun at Garibaldi's face. But he didn't seem to radiate the confidence such a position should entail. He looked scared . . . trapped.

Drake said, "There's a colony one jump from here. You're going to drop me off, and—"

"Why did you do it, Drake?" Garibaldi asked. "The Alliance went to bat for you, gave you the chance that nobody else back on Earth would give you. So why?"

"The Drakh made me a better offer," Drake said.

"And you don't care what they do to Earth as a result."

"Why should I? Earth never cared what happened to me. I say let 'em burn."

Garibaldi got up slowly, without making any sudden move that could set off the obviously jumpy Drake. He took a step forward, speaking very calmly.

"That's easy to say, Drake. Maybe even easy to do. Nice and impersonal. But pulling the trigger on that gun and turning my head into a canoe . . . You got the stones for that?"

"Stay away from me," Drake warned, panic lending an edge to his voice.

"Because," Garibaldi went on, "if you're gonna blow my brains out, you'd damned well better do it right now or I'm gonna tear your fragging heart out, Drake. And if you do shoot me, the rest of my people are gonna be all over you. What they'll do to you is worse than anything I could dream up in a thousand years. And I can dream real dark."

Drake's lips moved, but no sound came out. Then he managed to say, "I—"

The Minbari Ranger, who had been standing nearby all this time, as motionless as a statue, now started to make a move. Drake turned to fire on him. It was then that Garibaldi tackled him. They both went down hard. The PPG was knocked out of Drake's hand and skittered across the floor.

Garibaldi got up, pulling Drake up with him. He took great satisfaction in punching Drake then, and actually looked disappointed when the man collapsed into the arms of two Minbari Rangers.

Other Rangers had come to the bridge. They held Drake, who didn't resist.

"All right," Garibaldi said. "Now you're gonna tell me what the hell's going on here. You're gonna tell me everything you know . . . or I'm going to turn you over to them."

Drake glanced at the Minbari Rangers. He shuddered at the look of cold ferocity on their faces. Finally, he nodded.

—— chapter 45 ——

On *Excalibur*, Sheridan heaved a sigh of relief when the transmission resumed and Michael Garibaldi's image came up again on the screen.

"You were right, John," Garibaldi said. "After some convincing, our new friend has confirmed that the Drakh are heading right for Earth. They want to send a message to everyone else in the Alliance by wiping out Earth in a big show of force."

"And they may have a good chance of pulling it off," Sheridan said. "I just hope Lochley was able to convince Earth to mount a full-scale operation."

The navigation officer said, "We should be in Earth space any time now."

"All right," Sheridan said. Then, to Garibaldi, "Anything else?"

"Yeah, one piece of good news," Garibaldi said. "It seems the Drakh only have one Planet Killer—the only one the Shadows left behind. Of course, they don't want anyone else to know that, same way the United States didn't want anyone knowing they only had two atomic bombs when they went after Japan. But if we can stop this one, we won't have another one to worry about."

"Yeah," Sheridan said. "Well, we've still got to stop this one . . . and that won't be easy."

The navigation officer said, "Standing by, ready to enter Earth's space."

"I have to go, Michael," Sheridan said. "It's time. Get here when you can. If we fail, we'll need someone to pick up the pieces. Save as many of the survivors as you can—assuming anyone . . . Well, see you on the other side, Michael. *Excalibur,* out."

He turned to the navigation officer.

"Alert the *Victory,* and jump to normal space. Let's just hope they believed Lochley."

Outside, in space, two jump points formed up. *Excalibur* jumped, followed closely by *Victory*.

—— chapter 46 ——

If General Yuri Mikhail Denisovitch hadn't stopped off at the party for the new liaison officer from Minbar, everything would have happened differently.

Denisovitch would have been on his way to his dacha on the Karelian peninsula for a week's vacation. He would have spent most of the time in the projection room he had built in the back, next to the kitchen, where he could screen his Laurel and Hardy and Three Stooges movies. His communicators to the outside world would have been turned off. Denisovitch didn't take a holiday very often, and when he did, he didn't want to be disturbed.

So what would President Susanna Luchenko have done? Sent someone out to fetch him? Or authorized his second in command, the dolt Vasilevitch, a political appointee with no military experience, to act for him? In any case, valuable time would have been lost. And the result of that could have been catastrophic.

None of that happened, however. Denisovitch was at the party held in the reception room of the Hermitage in St. Petersburg. He was just toasting a luscious blonde from Budapest and making plans for her later—plans he hoped she'd agree to—when his aide, Dmitri Borisev, tugged at his sleeve.

"General. A call for you."

Denisovitch eyed his aide in a poignantly unfriendly manner. "I believe I told you, Dmitri, that my leave began twelve hours ago, and I am taking no calls until it is over."

"Yes, sir. You did. But this one is special. It is from President Susanna Luchenko."

The aide said this in awed tones. But Denisovitch was not impressed. He had always considered Luchenko somewhat too kittenish for serious business. And he knew she had a thing for him. She'd never come right out and said so, but he could always see the signs. She went for him in a big way. She just didn't know it. To encourage her, he sometimes made the first move himself. At these times he was severely rebuffed. A clear case of the woman's repressed side getting in the way.

"General . . ." His aide was growing agitated.

"Yes, all right, I'll speak to her." Then, to the blond Hungarian woman, he said, "My dear, excuse this minor interruption. Don't stir from this spot. I'll be right back."

The blonde nodded nervously. Denisovitch noticed that, even as he was crossing the room, she scurried off at once to find her husband. He regretted that she had been unable to cope with such an impressive and important person as himself.

Dmitri led Denisovitch to a little anteroom off the main reception area. The room was lined with shelves of old calf-bound books. It had a gold-threaded rug at least a century old. On an exquisite rosewood table sat a thoroughly modern workstation. In the monitor, the image of Susanna Luchenko loomed, waiting with poorly concealed impatience.

"Madame President!" Denisovitch said. "What a great pleasure! Have you changed your mind about joining me at the dacha?"

"As I told you, I can't make it," she answered, showing little patience for Denisovitch's ponderous gallantry. "And I'm afraid you're not going to make it, either."

"Why?" Denisovitch said, laughing. "Have I changed *my* mind?"

"You're going to have to. A situation has come up."

"Situations always come up," Denisovitch said. "It's in their nature. In a week, the matter will be more ripe to deal with."

"I don't think so," Luchenko said. "Listen, Yuri. I've just gotten word from John Sheridan. It seems that an enemy invasion fleet is on its way to Earth as we speak. We're going to have to scramble everything we've got, and we need to do it yesterday."

"An invasion fleet? Have some of our allies decided to attack us? I knew you made too hard a bargain at the last conference."

"This is no laughing matter," Luchenko said. "These are not friends. They're Drakh. And they're on their way. We need to put everything we've got into space!"

"All right, calm down," Denisovitch said, the humor draining from his voice. "What exactly did Sheridan say to you?"

"I didn't speak to him. Captain Elizabeth Lochley of Babylon 5 called in his place."

"Sheridan delegated the call? On a matter of this importance?"

"I asked about that, too. Lochley told me that Sheridan and one of his captains, a man named Anderson, are going to try to slow down the enemy fleet. They're in the two new prototype destroyers."

"Anderson? Are you aware that this Anderson went absent without leave, taking with him a major ship?"

"Of course I knew about that," Luchenko said.

"And that Sheridan has been acting increasingly erratic of late?"

"I know about that, too."

"Lochley must have been drunk to have called you that way," Denisovitch said. "Invasion? It's preposterous, a fantasy. Invasions don't come out of the blue. If there were anything to this, we'd have heard something."

"Lochley was not drunk."

"Did she witness this invasion herself?"

"No. But she said Sheridan had."

"So all she knew was what Sheridan told her?"

"Well, yes. Even so—"

"You are aware, of course, that some questions have been raised about Sheridan's competence."

"That's old news. He's been in the clear for years now."

"Haven't you seen the recent reports? Some of our agents have claimed that Sheridan is acting erratically, as though he is allowing some outside influence to direct him in his actions."

"He wouldn't be the first," Luchenko said. "Still, his claims must be seriously addressed. If there's even a possibility that Sheridan's warning may be true, we must act immediately. The alternative is unthinkable. I'm ordering you to scramble the fleet."

"No, Madame President," Denisovitch said gently.

"What? Are you refusing my order?"

"For your own good. The most likely explanation here is that John Sheridan has, as you would say, flipped out. It's not surprising, considering the stresses he's been through. Have you any idea what it'll cost to do what he's asking? And who do you think will be accountable for it? You will, that's who. I'm trying to save you from a serious mistake, Susan."

"And if Sheridan is right?"

"The likelihood is that he's wrong. Utterly, tragically wrong. The Drakh were on the losing side in our war against the Shadows. They're unlikely to have anything resembling a space fleet. I assure you, this is all some tragic figment in Sheridan's imagination."

He paused, then said, "At the very least, we should wait for more military intelligence."

"There's no time for that. This is too important, too vital for Earth's safety to permit any delay. If you won't act, you leave me only one recourse."

Denisovitch smiled. "To cancel this insane order and find out what is really going on? You can't force me to scramble the Earth fleet, you know."

"I know that. But I can relieve you of command."

"Madame President! You're joking!"

"I'm calling Vasilevitch as soon as we end this conversation. He'll take command while we select a new supreme commander."

"Dimitri? He's an incompetent. Susan, you *are* joking!"

"No, I am not."

Denisovitch took a deep breath. "You're really serious about this."

"I am."

"You think something like what Sheridan is claiming might actually be taking place?"

"I wouldn't be giving you orders now if I didn't!"

"Very well. I defer to your judgment, Madame President. I will scramble the fleet immediately. I just wanted to see how firm was your resolve."

"Well, now you know."

"Yes. I will get everything up as quickly as possible. And then we will see what is going on in Sheridan's poor crazed brain."

He cut the connection.

—— chapter 47 ——

From his vantage point in space aboard the *Hermes*, through special viewing equipment, General Yuri Mikhail Denisovitch could see the Earth, a small blue and white sphere. Between himself and the home planet, there was poised a huge array of ships, more than had been mounted before in recent memory.

The first elements of this armada, already space-borne, had moved into position less than two hours after Denisovitch had given his orders. The military dropped everything, canceled all port leave, put aside any repairs as long as the ships were spaceworthy, blasted off with whatever crews were available, and scrambled into position.

Most of these ships had assembled in space in less than five hours. There were the capital ships, the big battleships, cruisers, destroyers. Also there were all the rest of the ships Earth command had been able to mount: single-gun launches and tenders, outmoded models pulled out of retirement and launched into space. Scattered among them were a handful of White Star warships that had been visiting Earth on a good-will tour.

There were commercial ships as well, mingled with the EarthForce ships, trading ships from most of the industrialized nations of Earth, some without guns, without adequate armor. They had taken to space on their own initiative, once Sheridan's news had become generally known. The captains and crews of these ships knew they could do no more than interpose themselves in the battle to come, maybe saving a capital ship for further combat. There had been no argument about the correctness of what they were doing. Worst-case scenario called for them to die either in space, fighting, or on the ground, waiting for the end.

On Earth, the news had been broadcast planetwide on all media. It had been received with surprising calm. There just hadn't been time for panic.

Still, Denisovitch hadn't discounted the possibility that this was just a false alarm. It almost had to be! Surely an attack of the magnitude expected couldn't have boiled up as quickly as this. Soon it would all be over, they'd return to their bases, and the civilians would have something to boast about.

That's what he hoped, anyway. Because Earth really wasn't ready for the alternative.

He said into his comlink, "This is General Yuri Mikhail Denisovitch of the *Hermes*, to *Excalibur*, do you copy?"

Sheridan's image came up on the screen. "Confirmed, *Hermes*."

"We are all here . . . as you requested. But so far we have seen nothing."

"General—" Sheridan began.

Denisovitch cut him off. "Certainly, on behalf of the

Russian Consortium, which lost many of our citizens in recent conflicts, it is our hope that this exercise has—"

"This is no exercise," Sheridan said, breaking in.

Denisovitch was about to take issue, but at that moment an alarm began sounding on the *Hermes*. The officers around him on the bridge began chattering in Russian.

Denisovitch rose and went to the monitor.

"Good God . . . ," he said, backing up as though he had been physically struck.

The Drakh fleet had just been detected. It had come into view and was closing rapidly. Its advance was imposing, inexorable. Looking through the port, Yuri saw that the assault fleet was like a million tiny pinpricks of light, set out in rows that extended far past the limits of his vision. The dots were steadily increasing in size as they came closer. In their midst was the deathcloud, a monstrous octopuslike shape, its inky tendrils extending on all sizes like the wavy curls of a Medusa, larger than anyone could have imagined.

Sheridan said urgently, "General, listen to me. The fleet isn't our main concern. Leave them to the defense grid. The deathcloud itself is the real danger. They'll try to knock your fleet aside and position their Planet Killer where it can strike. You have to stop that from happening."

"What—what do you want me to do?"

"Captain Anderson and I stand the best chance of taking it out. Give us a flying wedge of ships to help punch a hole in their defense, and get us within striking range of that thing."

"And then what?" Denisovitch asked.

"Then we'll kill it," Sheridan said. He cast a mean-ingful look at Dureena. "Somehow."

General Yuri Denisovitch, in a sepulchral voice that sounded as if it had been summoned up from beyond the grave, said, "Good plan."

— chapter 48 —

The ensuing battle was a nightmare. Sheridan caught only glimpses of it, because he and Anderson had their own part to play, and couldn't afford the luxury of overseeing the efforts of others. Those opening seconds and minutes gave him only an impression of what was going on, but, he feared, an accurate one.

He saw the advance guard of the Drakh ships interpenetrate with the forward elements of the Earth fleet. Weapons fire sparked across space, arcing wherever a hit was made. In a mad confusion of enraged adversaries, the Drakh ships made no attempt to spare themselves. The ships from Earth, and the Alliance ships that had joined them in time, were equally adamant, equally berserk.

Sheridan caught a glimpse as two Drakh ships, cutting around in tight circles to avoid incoming fire, collided as they completed their circles. The ensuing explosion was like a nova, lighting up the sky for a moment before flaming out in the vacuum.

The ships from Earth were suffering, but Sheridan saw a group of four smaller ships—civilian vessels, from their size—zero in on a single Drakh ship and harry it through a series of tight maneuvers, their light weaponry making no real impression on the enemy. But they occupied his attention long enough for an Earth-Force destroyer to join the attack and, aided by his wing destroyer, make the kill. That was the good news.

Sheridan was also aware that the Drakh were cutting down Earth ships as fast as they could be put up, their armor, speed, and weaponry more than a match for Earth's best. Only *Excalibur* and *Victory* could slug it out with the Drakh on an equal footing, and both prototypes were engaged in an attack on the deathcloud.

Sheridan saw the thing looming ahead of him as he bore in on it. As he closed, he saw that it was larger than a planet; of course, since it was designed to engulf a planet. But there was no time to think of that. He drove *Excalibur* hard, grimly hanging on while his ship was rocked time and time again by incoming hits.

"Distance to target!" Sheridan demanded.

"Ten thousand miles!" his navigation officer replied.

"Fire forward guns, maximum power, wide dispersion pattern."

Control told him, "Sir, at this range the beams will disperse . . . They won't do any damage."

"I'm not looking to do any damage yet. I want to find out what that thing's made of."

"Aye, sir," control said. "Firing."

Excalibur was momentarily checked in its onward dash as it fired its main forward guns.

Sheridan tracked the volley on the tactical display. Some of the bursts penetrated the cloud and continued on into it, to explode deep in its interior. Other bursts passed straight through it.

"There," Sheridan said. "Some passed right through, others were stopped. That tells me there's a superstructure of some kind inside. If it's solid, we can hit it, and if we can hit the right spot, we can destroy it."

He wiped his forehead. This was hot work. He continued, "Scanners to maximum, full spectrum, starting at infrared and moving outward. Nothing we had before could ever penetrate that thing. Let's see how advanced this ship really is."

"Aye, sir," control said.

The display began showing shifting colors as *Excalibur* penetrated the outer edges of the cloud part of the deathcloud. Other screens, their cameras aimed aft, panned across the actions of the two fleets. They showed increasingly heavy damage being suffered by EarthForce.

And *Excalibur* seemed to take forever getting into the cloud.

"Come on," Sheridan muttered. "I could've painted this thing in oils by now."

"There!" Dureena cried.

They had finally penetrated the cloud deeply enough to reveal the superstructure that was concealed within it. It was a solid box of hinged steel, larger than Everest, an almost inconceivable product of evil but brilliant engineering, a juggernaut designed to crush a planet.

The great black metallic mass of long, spidery arms was moving through space, majestically, inexorably. A diffused light allowed Sheridan to pick up details of its missile array. There had to be thousands of the missiles in long racks within the superstructure, awaiting launch. And bad as that was to see, what was worse was that this great jointed mass of metal was expanding, opening up like a grotesque flower of evil, getting ready for the big one.

The crew of *Excalibur* was stunned for a moment by the sheer size of what they saw. The communications officer stood with his mouth open, printouts dropping unnoticed from his hand. Dureena had both fists clenched, and her body was a tense bow, as if somehow she thought she could hurl herself at this grim object. The navigation officer had lifted his hands to his face and now, somewhat sheepishly, was taking them down again and finding his voice.

He said, "My God! How are we supposed to stop something like that? It's as big as a planet."

"David and Goliath," Sheridan replied. "You just have to find the right point."

Dureena was listening to Sheridan's words, but her mind was far away. She was back on Daltron 7, in the dark, swirling place of the catastrophe. And she could hear Galen's voice again, as clearly as though he were speaking to her now, saying, "When the time comes to choose your target, be sure to pick the right one. Because you will get only one shot." She had thought he meant Sheridan, but . . .

She could see the display focusing in on the dead center of the jointed steel device. Sheridan had frozen the display.

"There," he said. "That has to be the control center; it's right in the middle of the thing. We hit it with everything we've got, and—"

"No," Dureena said.

Sheridan and the other officers looked at her, surprised by her intrusion.

"Excuse me?" Sheridan said.

Dureena was suddenly very sure of herself. "Hit that part, and you'll fail. And your planet will be destroyed."

They all clutched for support as *Excalibur* was rocked.

"Look," Sheridan said, "we don't have much time. We can't take too many more of those hits."

"Then listen," Dureena said. "Your friend was right about me. I'm a thief. And proud of it. I work like a thief, I live like a thief, and I think like a thief. So do they."

She paused to be sure she had their full attention. She had. Maybe they thought she was crazy, but they were listening.

"The first thing a thief learns is that the biggest jewels are never hidden in the safe. They're hidden in a box or book *next* to the safe. They're never in the obvious place, so you learn to look where they do not want you to look."

She walked up to the display and pointed to the center object.

"Maybe they assumed nobody could penetrate the deathcloud to its center. And maybe they did, in which case they'd know that the centerpiece would be the obvious target. So they reinforce it, but move the main segments of the control system elsewhere."

"Such as?" Sheridan asked.

Dureena studied the display, steadying herself and not even registering it as the ship took another hit.

"Here," she said, pointing to the screen. "Magnify."

Sheridan studied the image. It was a joint area located between fingers of the fist that formed the superstructure. It looked identical to all the other joints . . . except, as the image magnified, one very important difference became apparent.

"This looks like a joint between parts of the device," Dureena said. "Same as a thousand others. But if there's nothing special about it, then why all the short-range weapons surrounding it? Why are they so determined to protect it? If it's just one more joint in the mechanism, there's no reason for the extra weapons."

"Unless it's more than it appears," Sheridan mused, picking up her line of thought.

"Exactly," Dureena said.

Anderson's voice came in. He had been monitoring their conversation. "Sheridan. We're monitoring your situation. Enemy ships closing on our position. We're running out of time. We can hit one or the other, but not both. Whatever you're going to do, you'd better do it fast."

Sheridan looked at Dureena. She met his gaze steadily.

She said, "I wouldn't be here if there wasn't a reason, if I didn't have something to contribute. Maybe it's not a thing. Maybe it's a way of thinking."

She looked at him hard. "I know I'm right!"

Sheridan hesitated only a fraction of a second more. Then his mind was made up.

He said, "Engines at full! At weapons, prepare to fire as soon as we're within range."

"Which target?" the navigation officer asked.

"Hers!" Sheridan said.

The *Excalibur* seemed to take a running leap through space, *Victory* following, blasting away from the main group, still firing their other armament at the surrounding Drakh fleet. Beam weapons played across Drakh ships, letting off coruscating sparks. Incoming rounds exploded off Drakh hulls in a mounting dazzle of explosions. They raced away from their accompanying Earth destroyers, some of which were already on fire.

Closer and closer *Excalibur* came to the superstructure, weapons firing, hits coming in as more enemy guns began to bear on their targets. Behind them, the Earth was a pale-colored sphere barely visible through the cloud, swimming alone in the heavens, looking naked and vulnerable. And now *Victory* joined her firepower to *Excalibur*'s.

For a moment, Sheridan's maneuver looked as though it would work. But more and more Drakh ships came pouring into the area, adding their firepower, deflecting shots that had been aimed at the superstructure.

Aboard *Victory*, Anderson saw that they had been checkmated. He didn't need it when his first officer spelled out the obvious. "Weapon fire not getting through, Captain. Autodefense systems are bad enough, but we just had five more ships join in the defense."

"How long until it can hit Earth?"

"We're minutes away," the first officer said. And then he was thrown halfway across the bridge as the *Victory* took a solid hit in the rear.

The first officer picked himself up, face bloody, read his screen, and reported, "Main rear weapons are hit!"

"How bad?" Anderson asked.

"They're destroyed, sir," the first officer replied.

Anderson paused a moment. In his mind's eye, Earth was engulfed in a torrent of red death. Then he said, "My daughter's down there, Phil. I promised I'd protect her from the monsters. What kind of father am I . . . if I can't keep my promise?"

He thought for a moment, then said, "Get me Sheridan."

"Aye, sir," the first officer said.

——— *chapter 49* ———

Sheridan looked at Anderson's agonized face on the screen, heard him say, "Sheridan . . . standard weapons fire isn't getting through."

"I know," Sheridan said.

"Only one thing to do. Fire your main guns. It'll put you out of commission for one minute, but we'll cover you until you can navigate and get out of here."

"At this range," Sheridan said, "the most we'll do is knock out some of those ships."

"Exactly. But you'll clear the way so we can use our main guns, then you can cover *us*. Just open the door, Mr. President . . . We'll take it from there."

Sheridan looked at Anderson, a look that said a lot. Then Sheridan said, "Ready main guns. Stand by to fire."

The tension aboard *Excalibur* at that moment was almost unbearable. All of them on the bridge were caught up in their most private thoughts.

The navigation officer caught a memory glimpse of a small cottage in upstate New York, a place not far from Ausable Chasm, a place where, despite the rigors of the climate, roses grew, where a young woman waited for him, and a small boy waited, too.

Dureena caught a glimpse of the possibilities of life that lay ahead of her, a place for new memories, since her old ones had been obliterated along with her world.

It was the same with the others on the bridge. Each of them was caught up in a momentary flash of vision, a flash that told them how good life was, and how sad it would be to leave it now in a hell of molten metal and freezing vacuum. The moment seemed to stretch, to grow, lasting on and on . . .

Until Sheridan said, "Fire!"

The blast of the *Excalibur*'s main armament came crackling with the essence of living plasma. The beams from all four primary guns met in front of the *Excalibur* and shot out like a serpent's tongue, disturbing the fabric of space itself.

That fire, burning brighter than a thousand suns, consumed itself and flared up again as it screamed through space, exploding into a group of Drakh ships. This was the majority of the enemy force, hastily assembled to protect the superstructure behind them. In the blink of an eye, that great array of war vessels, with their well-wrought alloy bodies, optical-fiber nerves, computer brains, and their thousands of Drakh soldiers, was utterly consumed. It vanished from sight as though it had never been.

It was a signal victory, but a Pyrrhic one, as was apparent to everybody as they crowded around the screens. For *Excalibur*, plunged into darkness now as a result of the sudden expenditure of all her accumulated energies, had indeed maimed the Drakh fleet to the point of death, but had not touched the superstructure, protected as it was by so many Drakh ships and soldiers.

In the darkness, Sheridan remarked to Dureena, "Looks like you won't have a chance to shoot either of us."

Dureena shrugged. "I've grown accustomed to disappointment."

Suddenly the navigation officer cried out, "Sir! The *Victory*. She's breaking away!"

"What?" Sheridan said. He rushed to the window, looked out.

He saw *Victory*, side guns firing, racing toward the Drakh command center, picking up speed as she went.

Aboard *Victory*, Anderson gave his command.

"Ramming speed," he said.

"Aye, sir," the first officer said. He relayed the order to the engine room.

There was no reply. "Hey," he called. "Engine room, come on! Someone!"

Again a long wait. And then a voice made stupid with shock and pain said, "Engine room, Flagler reporting."

"Give me Lieutenant Dryson."

"Dead, sir."

"Then put on Sergeant Halloran."

"He's dead, too, sir. They're all dead. All except me. And I'm not sure of me."

The first officer read his dials. They were dipping toward the black. What a hell of a time to lose power. "Flagler?" he said urgently. "You've got to do something!"

"Yes, sir. I figured on dying next, sir."

"Flagler, listen to me! You can't die yet! Are you listening?"

Flagler heard the first officer's words, but he couldn't find anything to say. He lay in a corner of the engine room, where the explosion had flung him. On all sides of him were twisted metal and shattered bodies. Some of the eleven men present had been shredded by the exploding metal. Arms and legs lay scattered across the deck or plastered on the walls and ceiling. A jagged hole almost three yards long had been torn in the hull.

The air vents were huffing like a steam engine, laboring mightily to replace the escaping air that rushed out of the hull with an audible whistle. Automatic sealing mechanisms had already begun to work, laying down successive sheets of quick-drying film over the gap, trying to block it up.

Flagler observed all this dully, too shocked to react. Although he was splattered with blood and grease, as far as he could tell he wasn't badly wounded. Somehow the lethal shrapnel that had wiped out the crew had missed him. He was still alive. But he knew he wasn't going to be for long.

Unless he did something about it.

Already his mind was rehearsing the automatic procedures that had been drummed into him in training school, the procedures to follow when the ship was lost, but you were still alive.

Step one, get into a deep-space EVA suit. These were strewn all over the deck, having burst out of their storage locker when the engine room was struck. Several of them were shredded past repair, but at least one of them looked all right: it was a survivor, like him.

The thing to do was to get into the suit, then get out of the ship. That would be easy enough. He just had to dive through the film that was trying to form over the rent in the hull, but quickly, before it hardened.

That would leave him alone in space. The suit had only limited propulsive possibilities, but it had a broadcast beacon that could keep going for days, maybe a week. With a little luck, somebody would pick up the beam and rescue him. There was food and water in the suit. At least he'd have a chance.

It was the smart thing to do.

He heard a noise, became aware that it had been going on for some time. Someone was speaking to him.

"Lieutenant Flagler, can you hear me?"

Oh, yes, it was the first officer again. What was he going on about now?

"I can hear you, sir."

"The engines! We're losing the engines. Can you do something?"

It seemed a funny thing to be worrying about now. Nevertheless, Flagler pulled himself to his feet and picked his way across the deck to the engine room instrumentation. He studied the electrical layout diagrams that flashed red and yellow lines across a screen, with white *X*s representing breaks.

"Got some short circuits in there, sir. The strike must have messed up the circuitry."

"Damn!" the first officer said. "I guess we're dead in the water."

It was then that Lieutenant Flagler surprised himself.

What he had been going to say was, "Sorry, sir, it's a washout." Instead, he studied the board, and said, "No, sir, that's not the case at all. I can reroute the circuits as long as this backup board is still operative. Just a minute . . . There! Try that, sir."

Another moment's pause. Then, "Nice work, Flagler! We're able to power up. Maybe you'd like to come up here on the bridge and watch this."

"Watch what, sir?"

"A ship this size performing a ramming maneuver."

So that was it! They were all going to die. And he still had a chance. He thought of telling the C&C to go stick it. He'd read about it someday in the papers.

But he surprised himself again by saying, "I'd love to see it, sir, but I think I'd better stay here. In case any more circuitry goes down. Anyhow, I'll follow it on the monitor."

The small black-and-white screen mounted above the engine room instrument panel was still functioning.

"Okay," the first officer said. "Give us ramming speed."

Flagler punched in the command, heard the engines begin to roar. He settled back, watching his gauges.

He took one more look at the EVA suit. It was probably holed anyhow.

And so began the last ride of the *Victory*. She took hit after hit as she bored in. Tail fins and stabilizers were burned off her and came free in explosions of bright sparks. The ship kept on coming. A huge jagged hole opened in her waist, and another just behind it, wounding her mortally. But she kept on coming. A part of the front section blew away and tumbled free, itself the size of a small ship. The bridge hung precariously in place, but the ship was shedding parts, and it was just a matter of time, and not much time at that, before the diminishing domain of the Humans was pierced and exploded, too.

The lights flickered. Most of them went out. Only a few of the ready lights came on. The ship writhed with repeated impacts, all of them mortal blows. Anderson and his first officer exchanged looks. There was a strange calmness in that exchange, the look of understanding between men who have already spent their lives, who are dead already, but are hanging around just long enough to see the results of their actions and of their sacrifice.

Down below in the engine room, Flagler watched on the monitor, feeling intense satisfaction as the ship kept on moving, still gaining speed, boring directly toward the enormous jointed object that seemed to fill the whole sky. What a view! What a way to go! And it was his work that was carrying them to this!

And then the *Victory*, much diminished but still massive, blazing like a torch and shedding bits and pieces like some enormous insect molting in midflight, burst through a remaining screen of Drakh ships and struck the jointed steel platform with a blow that blew the Earth ship apart.

For a moment it didn't seem to do anything to the alien superstructure. That strange metal spiderweb absorbed the blow. Seemed to shrug it off. It was as though nothing had happened.

But that was only because it took a little time for irreversible processes to begin manifesting themselves. Then the superstructure began to judder and shake, slowly at first, then with greater speed, and the great jointed metal thing began moving, slowly at first, then faster and faster.

—— chapter 50 ——

Aboard *Excalibur*, Sheridan and the others on the bridge watched in silence as the *Victory* went to her doom. They were standing in darkness, lit only by the dials and the ghostly glow of the emergency backups. They were all stunned, contemplating *Victory*'s fiery end.

Sheridan in particular felt as though he had lost an old friend. Even though he had barely known Anderson, the rapport between them had been immediate and warm. Anderson's death was only the latest in the cruel blows his life of conflict had dealt him, first with the Minbari, then the Shadows, and now with their successors, the Drakh. He wondered when it would all end.

The minute of recharging seemed to go on forever, and Sheridan began wondering if anything in the ship would ever work again. He could almost feel the Drakh ships coming after *Excalibur*, preparing to strike while the ship's systems were down, blowing her to the same fiery hell that had engulfed Anderson and *Victory*.

At last the lights flickered back to life.

The navigation officer had been maintaining visual

contact with the structure within the deathcloud all this time. Now he said, "Sir . . . The mechanism . . . it's moving all around us . . . missiles active on all sides."

Sheridan replied, "The impact must have activated the mechanism prematurely."

He shook himself out of his momentary lethargy. It was time to be moving!

He said into the console, "Sheridan to fleet command, everyone clear out, I repeat, evacuate the area."

Then to the navigation officer, "Get us the hell out of here. *Fast!*"

Excalibur began moving, picking up speed. On the invisible three-dimensional chessboard of space, a strange deadly game was being played out.

The Shadow-built superstructure was moving with increasing speed, but erratically, obviously out of control, shaking itself apart and firing off its missiles as it moved. The deathcloud that surrounded it was conforming to its shape, following its direction, its long, snaky black tentacles reaching out and beginning to close.

The Drakh ships nearby were caught up in a situation they had never imagined or visualized. The Drakh ship closest to the deathcloud was hit and went up in a titanic, soundless explosion. Other Drakh vessels were scrambling to get out of the way, shooting off in all directions as if from the exploding core of a multiple fireworks display. And the Earth ships were deep into their turns and piling on the power, trying to escape the carnage.

Sheridan's ship was closest to the center of the carnage. At Sheridan's command, it spun on its heel and began streaking toward the Earth. The black tentacles of the deathcloud reached for it, overtaking it, trying to close around it.

"Faster," Sheridan said, watching as the tentacles began to come up even with *Excalibur*.

"This is as 'faster' as I can go," the navigator said through gritted teeth.

The contest between closing deathcloud and fleeing ship played itself out over the next few seconds, but it felt to those aboard *Excalibur* like several slow-motion years. Sheridan could see the dark fingers arcing over his field of vision, extending out in front of them, closing, striving to catch the ship.

Those fingers made their last reach and tightened. *Excalibur* was caught . . .

No, she got out of the closing fist just in time, preceded by several other Earth ships, all safe by the narrowest of margins.

Behind them, several Drakh ships, in close pursuit—but not close enough—burst into dazzling fireballs as the blind, giant fist tightened over them.

As the fist closed tight, all of the unexpended missiles fired simultaneously. There was a mounting wave of brilliance as the missiles went off, a searing flash of color across the spectrum. Photon-sensitive screens aboard *Excalibur* dampened down, to keep the crew from going blind.

The remaining elements of the Drakh fleet still within the zone of destruction were annihilated in another flash of unbearable brilliance, another wave of spectrum-covering color.

And the blasts went on, lighting up space like a galaxy of suns gone nova. Until at last the superstructure itself, damaged by *Victory*, swept by its own returning missiles, went up in an explosion that was like the first day of creation, or the last. The superstructure's long, thin spidery arms folded in on themselves. It looked like some creature of the night trying to claw itself to death. Sheridan could almost hear the shriek of outraged metal as it turned superhot and winked out of existence.

And then it was over.

Almost.

Because at that moment, the navigation officer, still blinking in an attempt to restore his full vision, said, "Sir . . . Look!"

Sheridan did, and felt a sudden stab of disappointment. He and Anderson had done the impossible, yet it hadn't been enough.

The deathcloud was gone. That much was indisputable. Space for thousands of cubic kilometers was filled with raining particles of steel. It should have been all over . . .

But elements of the Drakh fleet still remained outside the blast range. There were several of these ships, and one large one was in the lead.

They became the sole targets of the Earth defense grid. Brilliant lines of energy crisscrossed and swept toward them, and wherever energy lines crossed, an enemy ship winked out of existence.

But despite ongoing destruction from missiles and beam weapons, a few Drakh survivors continued to bore in toward Earth.

It took Sheridan a moment to figure out what they were doing. Was it a bombing run, or a strafing mission? No, they weren't loosing any bombs or beam weapons. But they were releasing something. He couldn't make out what it was.

He motioned to navigation to step up the magnification. He pressed his face against the port, willing himself to see what was going on, to understand.

At last light-diffraction telemetry showed him that these last few ships, which had penetrated into Earth's upper atmosphere, were releasing a spray.

Ground-based weaponry winked from the surface of the planet. EarthForce defenses picked the Drakh ships off one by one. The Drakh ships spiraled down out of control, crashing into the planetary surface. The big ship was the last survivor. Spitting defiance, releasing its spray, which glittered against the backlit burning hulks of its sister ships, it kept on moving. And then it, too, was shot down, exploding in the mother of all fireworks. But as it fluttered to Earth like a dying moth, it was still spraying.

Sheridan, realizing what had happened, sat down heavily, a stricken expression on his face.

"What is it?" Dureena demanded. "What happened?"

He looked at her. And she wasn't sure if she heard his words or imagined them.

"The Romans had a phrase for it," he said. "They called it 'poisoning the well.'"

Dureena stared at him, trying to take in the suddenly new situation.

"What they couldn't conquer," Sheridan explained, "they killed. When they were driven out of an area, they literally poisoned the wells, so no one else could live there, either."

—— chapter 51 ——

Later, he was explaining the same thing to Lochley, who, together with Garibaldi, sat gravely listening.

"It's the ultimate act of spite," Sheridan was saying. "If they can't have it, no one can."

Lochley asked, "Then they've finished analyzing whatever it was the Drakh sprayed into Earth's atmosphere?"

"It's a biogenetic plague," Sheridan said. "Earth has been completely quarantined. No one's allowed in or out. The deathcloud was the only one the Drakh had, but it wasn't the last weapon in their arsenal."

He shook his head, then went on. "From the complexity of its structure, the bioweapons division back home thinks the plague was probably engineered by the Shadows."

"How much time do they have?" Garibaldi asked.

"That's the only bright spot in this," Sheridan said. "Apparently the Drakh didn't have time to finish adjusting it to our biology . . . or maybe they just didn't know how. Either way, it's going to take time for the plague to adjust to a new host. They're saying five years, but that's just a guess. Could be less. And some people may be affected by it sooner than others. But five years seems a pretty good guess for now."

"And at the end of five years?" Lochley asked.

"Every man, woman, and child on Earth will be dead. Unless they can find a cure."

Garibaldi said, "If the plague was created by Shadow technology centuries ahead of our own, how are they gonna solve it in five years?"

"They can't," Sheridan said flatly. He stood up. "But since this thing came to us from outside, then maybe we can find a cure for it out there. We know there were other races as old as the Shadows. One of them must have found a cure. We'll find them. We have to."

Outside the port, Sheridan could see helmeted men working on Babylon 5's hull. Several White Stars were moving in to dock.

He said, "I've told President Luchenko that we'll put all the resources of the Alliance, and the White Star fleet, at their disposal. We'll turn the *Excalibur* into a traveling research vessel, manned by the best crew we can find. The Rangers will search every corner of space, looking for clues to a cure. Then the *Excalibur* and her crew will go in to follow it up."

He paused a moment, then said, "Legend said that one day the real Excalibur would return in our greatest hour of need. I guess this is it."

"What about the rest of the new fleet you were building?"

"The Drakh hit the construction dock on their way out," Sheridan told her. "Years of work, wiped out in a second. We'll start over, but it'll take time. Until then, the *Excalibur* is the only one of her kind."

* * *

As Sheridan was talking, outside, a curious-looking black ship emerged from a jumpgate. Unlike most spaceships, it had large wings and a stabilizer. It was evidently designed for atmosphere as well as vacuum.

Sheridan said, "Those who command the *Excalibur* will never stop, never give up, and never slow down until a cure is found."

The curious-looking ship docked at a B5 entry port. A cloaked man emerged and entered the station.

At Babylon 5 customs, Dureena was hanging around, following a presentiment she didn't really believe but had found impossible to ignore. It had held her here for hours. And now she saw why.

Galen came walking through the customs barrier.

Sheridan was saying, "And we'll take any help we can get, wherever—and whoever—it comes from."

"I was hoping to see you," Dureena said to Galen. "In fact, I expected you. I just didn't know what I was expecting."

"We never do," Galen said, with a smile.

"Does this mean the techno-mages are working on our side?" she wanted to know.

"Let's just say *I'm* working on your side," Galen said. "That will have to suffice for the moment."

"So where to now?"

Galen considered for a moment and smiled. "Have you ever been to Mars?"

"No," Dureena said. "Where is it?"

"Nearest the heart of the fire," he said, and began walking.

She hurried to follow, sure somehow that she would be doing this for quite some time to come.

In Lochley's office, Sheridan said, "This is a cause that surpasses borders and differences. This is a mission about the survival of Earth itself. What we do over the next five years, here, at home, and across the darkness between the stars, will determine whether an entire world will live, or die. It's a fight we can't afford to lose. And we won't. We won't."

ANNOUNCING
THE PAST, PRESENT,
AND FUTURE OF...

ALL NEW EPISODES
BABYLON 5: THE FIFTH SEASON
WEDNESDAYS 10PM (ET)

THE SERIES: SEASONS 1-4
BABYLON 5
MONDAYS-FRIDAYS 6PM (ET)

Look for all the *Babylon 5* books.
Published by Del Rey Books.

*Del Rey proudly presents a five-book set
of definitive episode guides to the smash-hit
SF TV series!*

Babylon 5:
Season by Season

Book 1, **SIGNS AND PORTENTS**, features: a foreword by actor Michael O'Hare (Commander Sinclair); two introductory essays—"Getting *Babylon 5* into Orbit" and "*Babylon 5*'s First Season"—by author Jane Killick; a complete synopsis of each episode, from the pilot, "The Gathering," through the climactic season finale, "Chrysalis," followed by an in-depth analysis.

Book 2, **THE COMING OF SHADOWS**, includes: Killick's essays "By Any Means Necessary: Making *Babylon 5* on a Budget" and "*Babylon 5*'s Second Season"; a complete guide to and analysis of the season's twenty-two episodes, including "Points of Departure," "Hunter, Prey," and "The Fall of Night."

Book 3, **POINT OF NO RETURN**, begins with a fascinating look at how this groundbreaking series pioneered a new special-effects frontier. Then Killick's essay "*Babylon 5*'s Third Season" presents a thrilling summation of the series' major turning point—the culmination of the Shadow War. And episode-by-episode summaries cover all of the third season's twenty-two shows, including the stunning finale, "Z'ha'dum."

Book 4, **NO SURRENDER, NO RETREAT**, sums up the spellbinding fourth season: Captain Sheridan being pronounced missing and presumed dead on Z'ha'dum, Delenn feverishly rallying support for an all-out offensive against the Shadows, internal strife among the Centauri erupting in a shocking and violent betrayal, and Garibaldi resigning as security chief and plotting against his comrades. From "The Hour of the Wolf" to the shattering finale, "The Deconstruction of Falling Stars," Jane Killick's summaries and analyses capture all the action and intrigue of Babylon 5 circa 2261—"the year everything changed."

Book 5, **THE WHEEL OF FIRE**, covers the last season of the history-making show as the action reaches the boiling point and the stage is set for the new follow-up series, *Crusade*. Episode by episode, Jane Killick looks at Byron and his rogue telepaths' demand for a homeworld, Elizabeth Lochley's assignment as head of Babylon 5, Sheridan's inauguration as president of the new Alliance, G'Kar's unwilling ascension to the role of messiah, and the clandestine political intrigue on Centauri Prime. (Available April 1999)

Babylon 5:
Season by Season

Published by Del Rey Books.
Available wherever books are sold.